S0-ABE-237

Dedicated to

Kanvi Evans

Always Believe in your Dreams.

Always Love Ya.

W. P. Evans
(Wayn)
G-PA

11-24-16

SEARCHING FOR THE GOOD WAR

Can One Lone Man Alter the Destiny of the Entire World?

By W. D. Evans
The Man with More Lives Than a Cat™

To all those in my family who always helped me believe that my impossible dreams could come true.

To my Grandson, Benjamin Smitty, who tirelessly listened to my many adventures and told me I had lived more lives than a cat. Thus, to his credit, I became

"The Man with More Lives Than a Cat." ™

Warning

This is not a story - it is a journey!

It is **NOT** a journey for the Politically Correct masses, with their 30-second clips and sidebars. It's a call to those select few who have their own dreams with visions of a better tomorrow and the courage to tell the world of doubters *It's All Right to Be Different* and to *Be Happy with Who You Are.*

This is a Raw Journey

It is a Journey to be Not Told, but Lived, in his World of Lies, Spies and Wild Arctic Beasts.

It is a World of Murder, Hate, Love, Guilt, Passion, Fear, Fantasy, Regret, Forgiveness, Rebirth.

It is a Journey where rules do not exist, No Correctness, No Polish, No Respect for Convention.

It is a Journey of a struggling young man where there is No Time or Place for Proper Order.

It is a Journey of Searching for Answers to an Entire Life of Questions when there may be none.

With Unconditional Love, Can one Lone Soul Alter the Destiny of the Entire World?
Can there be a True, Good War?

As it is with his Real Life of Chaos, so it is with his Journey into Arctic Hell.

Expect Nothing but Raw Confusion, Nothing More, Nothing Less. I know of his Life of Struggles.

For it is My Journey,
"Searching for the Good War."

W. D. Evans
The Man with More Lives Than a Cat ™

Dedication

Only those who survive war know of its true terror. Their worst nightmare is their constant reality, the plague of the valiant warrior, Post-Traumatic Stress Disorder (PTSD). Plagued by this disease of the mind, they are forced to live over and over the worst nightmare of their mortal lives.

I, too, was in the service, the U S Army, and along my life's path of more than 80 years have experienced over 24 life-threatening events. Being threatened by polar bears and attacked by a herd of stampeding caribou, even crashing airplanes four times, are just a few of life's challenges I desperately try to forget, but then realize they are agonizing tests of my will to live and go on. Still, at times, these nightmares become my life of constant darkness.

To those who suffer from our PTSD, I dedicate this book, *Searching for the Good War,* with its message to: live each day of loneliness with hope for a better tomorrow, have faith in yourself and a greater power, believe in all those you care for and those who care for you, and always remembering to take an extra big spoonful of the greatest of all medicines to conquer your fears—Unconditional Love.

While *Searching for the Good War,* I too am forced to relive my own Post-Traumatic Stress Disorder, and Dark Visions of "The Slaughter of War."

Respectfully Submitted,

W. D. Evans

Prologue

Wayne, like all humans, has spirits who have watched over him from the time he was born. Some come with love and life to help him. Others come with hate and death to destroy him. Most of the time we are not seen or heard. However, there are times our work in his life has been evident. He can see the result of our presence, feel our touch, and hear our voices deep within his mind.

Not long ago I had a physical form, but now I am a special spirit to aid Wayne during his growing time of need. Whenever I appear to him, he must know me only as the guardian angel for which he has always prayed. I must be the father figure he can trust and have faith in, his spiritual father. I know firsthand of his struggling life of yesterday, his fear of love today, his uncertain tomorrow, and his hatred of his true, deserting father.

For now, I must conceal my true identity from Wayne until the right time. No matter who I truly am, my spirit still comes to him from the light side of his searching mind, with the love of a true father. It is my mission to help him tell this story of his impossible journey, to guide, to teach, and protect him, even from himself.

For his own salvation, I must continue to only be his friend, Michael, the father of those who have no father, the keeper of lost souls, the redeemer of Impossible Dreams. It is only when he has earned his final deliverance from his dark side that he may discover the truth of who I am, for it is only then that "the truth will set him free."

For more than a year, Wayne will be on a mission, not only to safeguard the United States' national defense system, but also to discover who he really is, and what his personal mission in life may truly be. During his constant search for the secrets of War, Wayne must learn to conquer his real and imagined fears and how to draw upon the courage he does not yet know he already has.

To help guide him on his treacherous journey, he will

only be armed with his Free Will and clues given to him as needed by the holy spirits in his battles to survive his frightening world of Lies, Spies, and Wild Arctic Beasts.

My Slaughter Begins

Born into poverty, my life has not changed much, even into my early twenties now. I have never had real family, love, or joy. For me, true friends are few and far between, and must be cherished as a priceless diamond and caressed with every ounce of my dying strength as my new life of hated slaughter begins.

It's the late 1950s. I have just been hurled into this new world of global chaos. The Cold War is boiling over. The US Navy is boarding suspected Russian spy ships in the Arctic Ocean. In retaliation, the Russians are shooting down US high-altitude spy planes flying over Russia's most-secret military installations. As a prelude to invasion, Russian bombers are poised to fly over the North Pole, ready to attack the northernmost US Arctic national defense radar systems. This frigid hell is where a nuclear holocaust will either start or be stopped before it ever begins.

Along with countless other privates, I have been drafted into the military in preparation for this terrible War, a giant bird of prey, perched on the edge of total world annihilation. In just three months of this frigid hell, I must be trained to "kill or be killed" and will be forced to honor the dark demon god of Slaughter, WAR.

Here, at the Fort Benning Army Training Center in South Georgia, the winter is not yet over, but the torrents of early spring rain have already turned the solid earth of bricklike clay into perpetual mud. As with the other young, frightened Army grunts around me, I am forced to realize this is not a night of pretend games, for just beyond our darkening horizon looms the threat of yet another holocaust of War.

To prepare us for our role in this world of chaos, we are forced to face the screech of flying bullets and deafening concussions of exploding bombs. We have been told the bullets must be real to help us fully understand the dangers of War and the importance of doing as we are told by our commanding officers. There is no room for mistakes in battle, so there must be no mistakes in our training. I am afraid, yet I cannot escape this trauma all around me.

Struggling to crawl only inches at a time, my body jerks back as I feel the sting of the same barbed wire that ranchers use to hold back wild cattle, wire tearing at my blood-soaked clothes and slicing, again and again, into my still young flesh. I shudder at the thunderous roar of the bombs violently exploding in foxholes, spewing out geysers of the smelly, stagnant winter rain. The pulsing sounds of machine guns vomit out their endless tracer bullets, creating a stream of Haley's Comet trails. Just inches above my head, glowing streaks of death light up the cold, pitch black Georgia sky. In all this turmoil, I must honor an impossible demand to keep my rifle dry. For I do not know, some dreadful day, I may be called upon to shoot or even cut to pieces my attacking enemy. He may be a soldier who's even younger than I, even my feared foe, a Russian.

Crawling just ahead of me, covered in the same putrid mud, is my best friend, George. He is already a hero in my eyes. Turning his head, I can see George yelling, "Hey, Evans, keep your butt down, or you're gonna get it shot off!"

George is totally fearless, with the courage I can only imagine discovering within myself someday. Yet, after almost three months together, I have discovered my fearless friend is afraid of one earthly creature. No mere human, but greasy, slimy Snakes. Another bomb explodes so close that I can no longer hear it. Instead, as a wild beast of War, its concussion roars deep within my bones.

George suddenly slips and kicks more mud into my face. He then struggles to look back at me.

Between the deafening explosions, he shouts, "Sorry, Little Brother."

After this eternity of swimming in frigid, winter mud together, my friend suddenly stops. For us, time now stands still. Of our many months of training together, the past hours, days, even weeks, become nothing but an instant of evil silence overcoming our world of Hell. He panics when suddenly one of his slimy enemies squirms up against him and strikes. I know George well. I know what he will do now, what he must do. As if to force me to take part in this deadly battle for life, this demon of slimy mud holds back my struggle to grab my friend's slippery boots. I miss.

Before my angry eyes of failure, George instinctively jumps up to run. He looks back at me and screams his last word on earth, my name, "Wayne!" as he is violently cut in half by the relentless streams of burning machine gun bullets.

For an instant I stop breathing in total disbelief, then gather just a fragment of the great courage my friend once had, just seconds before. Forcing my quivering lungs to cry for help, but with only the light of streaking bullets to pierce the darkness, we cannot be seen. My feeble voice cannot be heard over the deafening noise of exploding bombs. But my brain demands I try to get help, even though I know my friend is already dead. Even in death, George tries to protect me from the numbing cold. His warm, bloody remains blanket my shivering body.

My mind tries desperately to reverse the clock of time to these past few moments of life together and my desperate struggle to save my friend, but once again, I fail. His slaughter is my perpetual guilt for which I shall live in Hell, until finally meeting my own demon of death. Mixing blood with blood and flesh with flesh, as if a true family of blood brothers, I know we now have a bond of friendship that I must keep the rest of my life.

Still deaf from the concussion of exploding bombs, I vow to survive and honor the memory of my best friend, my Army buddy, "Private George," for all Eternity. I must discover the dark soul of War and learn the secrets of how to conquer it. For now, I am still alive. But what of George? For George, there is no tomorrow. No first leave to go back to his loved ones. No chance to be that officer others believed he could be. No life, No love, No children's laughter. Just a government letter of an unavoidable training accident and regret.

The Bomb's concussion is still just as real, the Bullet's pain still just as real, the Red of Blood still just as real. War, or just training for War, it is still just as real. My beloved friend Private George is still just as...Dead!

Yet, covered in George's blood, I still live. With the roar of bombs echoing in my brain, this glowing stream of slaughter comes searching for its next victim...ME!

WAR Lives

In fear, anger, and desperation, I cry out, "Oh GOD, How I Hate War! Oh GOD, after the slaughter of all those I love, how I Hate War! Damn you. Damn you to Hell!"

"Wayne, Murderer of Friends! You called me?" the dark, cruel beast answers back.

"That was a curse, not a call. Who or what are you?"

"I am the father of all your guilt, fears and hate. I come from the dark side of your subconscious mind."

"You are not real, just another vision of my tortured past."

"True, Wayne, so very true, but you asked who I am. What name do you hate the most for killing all you have ever loved?"

"WAR!"

"Then that's what you can call me...Mister WAR."

"No, never Mister, just cruel, bloody **WAR.**"

WAR, who lives through forces of evil, knows he will have to battle all the forces of good Wayne possesses—Free Will, Friendship and, above all, Love. These are powers Wayne does not know he has yet but, thanks to WAR, he soon will.

By responding to Wayne, WAR has unwittingly opened the door to Wayne's light side and launched the very beginning of Wayne's hidden powers to subconsciously communicate with spirits of good for help in battling his evil, dark side.

Infuriated, WAR makes his threat very clear, "Wayne, I warn you, I have come to discover your strengths, weaknesses, fears, and doubts! So, I *will* defeat you in our battles for your mortal soul. Flee as you may try, you cannot escape from a world of your own making, your world of endless darkness, your world of perpetual guilt for murder."

WAR's disgust for Wayne continues to grow. He tells

Wayne everything he has learned by watching Wayne since the day he was born.

"When you were one-year-old your father deserted you and your family, and you were thrust deep into poverty during the Great Depression. As I intended, you learned to hate your father and banished him to the darkest part of your mind forever, forgetting he ever existed. Soon, your mother met and married Steve, a man with boundless love, even for children borne of another man. He was the only man you ever called 'father.' But, War was on the horizon, and Steve joined the US Navy, where he and I met in the most disastrous way imaginable. Steve was at Pearl Harbor when the enemy thrust the United States of America into World War Two. That is when his slaughter, at War with me, began and soon ended. Another life and love lost to me.

"Within six years after the Second World War ended, a War began in Korea. Your older brother was called to serve—drafted—and he went with both pride and fear. Your brother was killed in that War, and your mother received another 'Killed in Action' letter. By this time, you had come to truly hate War and Death, but were later drafted as well.

"You had no spiritual training, no formal religion to plead your case against War. So, five years after your brother's death you answered your nation's demand that you, too, risk your life in War. I was out to get you, first through the deaths of your family, and then through the loss of your own soul to Death.

"However, I did not succeed in taking your life. Instead, my first attempt ended with the loss of George, your best friend and brother-at-arms. Much to my surprise, and joy, you remained in deep depression and guilt over not saving George. I knew you would feel helpless and planned to torment you until the day I finally eased your burden of Guilt through Death.

"Since everyone you ever cared for was taken from you in tragic, senseless War, you became frightened for those you may later try to love. You believed it to be your perpetual curse to be the right hand of the dark Demon of Death, WAR. Nevertheless, you vowed to find a way to defeat me at any cost.

"Admit it. You deserted your best friend when he needed you the most. He died a horrible death. I know, for I was there, deep in the shadows of those blazing, screaming shells. Why did you not try harder to save him, again and again? Oh, I know all about your stupid dreams of inner peace, riches, and finding eternal love but you won't find them in this ever-deeper pit of guilt you have dug for yourself. As with your friend, your dream of a better tomorrow is also dead. For all eternity, for your failure to protect you brother, you will rot in your black world of fear and guilt and relive your sins forever. You are Guilty of not just murder, but that of your best friend." With these final words, WAR leaves Wayne to wallow in the misery of his own dark thoughts.

Post-Traumatic Stress

Without warning, for endless days and nights, my life of terror and unfulfilled love explodes from my struggling subconscious mind and forces me into an eternal War to battle my damning, evil dark side of guilt and fear. Must this be an endless search deep within my very soul for even a tiny ember of light to guide me on some yet unknown path to redemption? Must my future of perpetual chaos be my only guide, praying for a time of healing, a time to live again, a time to love once more?

With visions of his past, and the guilt of causing his friend George's death, Wayne is thrown back into this violent memory again and again. Such is the personal hell of the damned, the curse of thousands who must forever live in their tortured world of yesterday.

Plagued by this disease of the mind, they are forced to live over and over the worst nightmare of their mortal lives. It is not their vivid imagination. Not even a three-dimensional hallucination, but a journey back into their warped past. It's an explosion of every human sense, to see, to hear, to smell, to taste, to touch, to struggle again with every trauma of their dark world of terror, the world of the forgotten, valiant warrior, the dark, cold, lonely world of the subconscious mind called Post-Traumatic Stress.

Wayne tries to fight the memories through the power of his mind.

No, I cannot, I must not, go back there again and again into these terrible nightmares of my agonizing past and my hatred of WAR. Not after all these months of constant battles with my mind just to regain some

small measure of sanity. When will these demonic visions end, or will they ever?

The battles to just survive this life of terror, projected into my brain, must end soon, or I too must die. If this must be my fate, through my mortal death I may seek out the home of my dead friend's heavenly soul, there to plead for his forgiveness and for my redemption. The peace I have craved for so long has died, buried with the blood and slaughter of my friend.

We were trained to be a team, protecting each other when and where our duty called. Together we were to forge a new world of love and peace. I failed to protect you when you needed me the most. I destroyed our dream. You sacrificed your life, in vain. I caused your death, the slaughter of my blood brother, my eternal friend, George. I am truly guilty of your murder.

George, is this all true? Did I truly desert you and cause your death? Must I believe I am guilty of murdering you as I did our friendship?

"Wayne, I am still your friend, as you are mine, and I will forever remember you. The demon of darkness and death, the one you call WAR, fears only Free Will, Truth, Friendship and, above all, Love. These are your ever-growing swords to battle against his lies and fear. Your Friendship has saved me. Not my earthly life, but my eternal being, my soul. Somewhere in time we shall meet again. For right now, though, your deeds of destiny must be fulfilled and your gifts to mankind bear nourishing fruit for all the ages to come. I must leave you now, but only for a little while. Fear not, Wayne, my little brother, I will always be in your heart."

Don't go, George. Help me remove this perpetual guilt of your death from my soul and be my aid in my redemption. Please Don't Go!

First Dance

Even in the midst of confusion, turmoil and chaos, Wayne still tries to believe there is a reason for him to live. He desperately begins the search for his personal mission, even in the midst of all his struggles just to exist. On his journey for truth, in those few moments of conscious reality while on his first leave from the army, he is compelled to attend a local dance. There, as if by a mystical plan of nature, he meets the companion and soul mate for whom he has searched during so many years of loneliness. Her name is Ann, a young office worker of 19, not even out of her teens. She is uncommonly attractive, but she does not yet believe in her beauty, nor in her own capacity to love, the growing love that will be Wayne's hidden strength in his many battles against his dark side.

Her friends call her Annie. Annie lives in a stable world of "average." She was born into a middle-class, hardworking, Midwestern family. She has average wants in life: find an average man to marry, have an average family of her own, make enough to afford an average home, and live an average life.

But, this is not her life to be, for her dancing partner is Wayne, a serviceman, home on his first leave. He is barely out of his teens at 21 but, to her, he is an older, mature man. He is tall, slender, and reasonably good-looking, even handsome, in Annie's eyes. As they listen to the music, they talk and dance, holding each other so very close. Is it a chance meeting or is it their destiny?

Unlike Annie's world of a loving family, Wayne lives in a world of chaos, suspended between Reality and Fantasy. His life of terrifying visions began as a mere child of one, when he first blamed himself for his father's desertion. He believes he could never be a good father and so has avoided love and marriage. He lived almost his entire young life with both guilt and a constant fear of poverty. His mind desperately searched for a perfect father to guide him, real or imagined. With all of this and the guilt of George's violent death constantly exploding in his struggling mind, he suffers through his traumatic battle silently and alone. He has struggled all his life to hide the plague of shame and guilt from others, even while searching for someone to understand and help in his healing.

Yet, as if by a blessing from above, Wayne and Annie find each other. As the opposing forces of the poles of the earth join to bind the dust of the universe to create one world of strength and life, so it is with these two souls from opposite worlds. They are destined to join their different lives as one, to rescue each other and create their imagined, bright new world together.

Their real world of the late 1950s is far from average in their search for Eternal Love. It is one of constant Threats and Fears. Threats of another World War, even worse than what they remember from their childhoods, with the justified Fear of a world-ending nuclear holocaust. Together, they will be thrown into this world of chaos, where they must do their part to save their world from global disaster, a world they have both been violently forced to join. They must learn to battle their personal War. They must earn their Eternal Love.

Wayne is joyous over their meeting, but has deep concerns about what he may have done to the simpler life of his new love, Annie. He feels that among their times of joy there will be many times of sadness for her as she becomes part of his chaotic life, a life he vows to change to earn her love.

At last, with a reason to exist, to be worthy of Annie's love, I must search for a way to overcome my life of poverty and discover my true self, away from shame and guilt. I know it will be a desperate journey, and along the way I pray I will find George's forgiveness for my failing to save him from his horrible death. Yes, my good friend George is dead, but I can still feel him deeply within my very heart and soul, and I try to remember our times of joy together. But, where to begin on this treacherous road to my final freedom? For now, I must live with these constant nightmares of slaughter and blood when all I long for is the warm, beautiful world of spring and love to come alive in my heart once again. For now, I must believe in finding a world at peace someday and trying to create a magical life with my Eternal Love, Annie, free from poverty and guilt.

Visions

Wayne shortly returns to his military career. He has learned his trade of death well. Outwardly, he appears to be a successful soldier, but because of his constant emotional guilt and traumatic visions from the past, he believes himself to be unworthy of Annie's love. With these added regrets, he creates within himself constant episodes of even greater Post-Traumatic Stress, which he has learned to hide from all others, except his new love.

Over many months, mostly apart while he is back in the army, Wayne vows he will find a way to earn Annie's love by discovering a path to a sane mind, destroying his poverty, and avenging George's death from War.

As he has done many times before, the demon of War and Fear appears and taunts Wayne with even greater regrets and guilt. During this emotional trauma, Wayne calls out for the miracle of a second chance to save his friend Private George, now long dead. But, there is no answer. As true as these visions appear at the time they occur, his conscious mind of reality will not remember them. Left with only his dramatic emotions of the encounters, he feels both happy and afraid, but does not yet understand why. In his search for some inner peace, in his dreams, even Annie comes back to him with her memories—some fond, yet others frightening—as she ponders her new life of uncertainty after falling in love with Wayne, her "Soldier Boy."

Memories and Letters

Annie Remembers

Wayne, I loved our dancing together on this marvelous 5th of May, the night that fate brought us together. At our beautiful Danceland, you and I were enjoying a simple soda.

In a funny way I thought of this as our first imaginary date. You told me you were heading back to New Jersey in a couple of days and asked me to go out with you the next day. I slightly paused, but not too long, and said that I would love to go on a date with you. A real first date. I was in 7th heaven and still couldn't believe how my life changed in an instant.

I wondered why this all began to happen to me, and why I fell for you so quickly. To start with, you were tall, which I really loved because I always wore three-inch heels and most guys I had dated were then shorter than I was. I could now truly look up to someone who was tall and oh so handsome. That was a big plus in my book.

As hard as it was for me to believe, I fell in love with you, Wayne, my Soldier Boy, from the first moment we danced and you held me so close. Being a soldier on limited leave, we had time for just one date, but one was all we needed.

The next day we went to a drive-in movie, a real date at last. I promised my sister and my friend I would be very proper and sit on my side of the car, which I did. As my new Soldier Boy you then did just as I hoped and sat right next to me, very close. Oh, that was so nice. You were this older man of 21 and I was a young girl of just 19. What a perfect match we would make, I thought. Well that was the end of my going to Danceland, or even accepting any more dates with anyone but you.

I knew just who I wanted to be with now, even though you were soon to be so far away in New Jersey, next to New York. I soon stopped buying all those expensive dresses from the little dress shop in Hammond, Indiana, and started to save my money, just in case we needed it someday.

Because of his new secret radar and communications system training in the Army, Wayne is taught well how to Lie and Deceive. This goes against all he has been taught to believe in—Honesty and Truth. But in this new world of enemy espionage and spies, his special knowledge puts him, his loved ones, and his country in jeopardy if he were to ever break his silence on what he knows of national defense systems.

Not knowing about this new world of secrets Wayne must now live in, Annie tries her best to understand his growing silence towards her by his not writing.

During this silent time of no letters from you,

and not knowing any of your struggles, I believe you must have been totally dedicated to your new military life, and that you also needed some time to think about what your later civilian life might hold for you. I pray it to be a life with me.

Truly believing that Wayne would not just abandon her without reason, Annie buries her young pride and boldly acts to find an answer.

I finally mailed you my letters and very soon I received the first of many letters from my Soldier Boy once again. Our new growing correspondence began our many years of ever-closer bonding and love—my Unconditional Love.

The Return

Two years finally pass, and with all his military awards Wayne is honorably discharged back to civilian life. Outwardly, he continues to appear to be a very successful and stable soldier who has done his duty for his country. Yet, inside he feels it is just a façade to mask his ever-growing struggles with his traumatic visions of the past. Wayne is already living with his eternal blame for his father's desertion, George's violent death, and the death of all those who were slaughtered by WAR. Added to all this, because of his burden of government secrecy, he has to continue to lie to everyone, not only about his past, but about his new life of secrecy. Worst of all, he has to abandon his commitment of honesty to his beloved Annie.

He has not yet learned of Annie's deep wisdom of human understanding and her true and growing love, a love that will be his inner strength in his many battles yet to come.

After almost two years apart, you finally came back and at last proposed to me. After a pause—a very short one—I said yes. You then gave me a very special engagement ring. It was your mother's ring, given to her by her precious love, lost in the terror of War. I still wear it to this date and it is the most beautiful ring in the world since it carries so much true love, our love.

Together again, yes, but the reality of my new life soon shows its ugly head. Many desperate months have passed since George's terrible death and my release from active duty, yet meaningful employment is not mine to have. Even though all the knowledge I earned while in the Army is still of value to the military, these same talents are of little use in my new civilian world. It is now a world of unbelievable struggles. I am just a penniless veteran, as are so many others of my generation. This new world of mine does not ask, but demands, a real job with real money, just to exist. I do not have either one, not even enough to buy a marriage license. I now believe this impossible dream of our eternal love may no longer be our destiny in life.

With the stress of having no job and the fear of constant poverty, Wayne feels unworthy of Annie's love. The perpetual threats of his hated WAR once again violently saturate his traumatic mind with visions of his world of slaughter and death. Instead of being at peace, the world he returns to is in global turmoil.

Then, as if by a miracle from above, a letter arrives from a clandestine government agency. Wayne is offered a position, not as a soldier, but as a well-paid secret agent on a critical mission of national defense using the same specialized military skills his civilian life has long rejected. But, he has to accept this government offer within a 90-day window, before a special training session in Alaska begins.

Once again, as in the Army, he will be in total isolation from his new loved one and his family. With his Free Will he is forced to make an impossible decision. He could choose to remain at home, close to those he loves, and continue his almost impossible search for some job with starvation wages. This is the easier but terrible choice, knowing his life would be one constantly plagued by the threat of poverty, in a world of regrets, failure, and everlasting guilt. His Impossible Dream of a brighter future would then constantly struggle to just survive and would ultimately die a whimpering death, along with his Eternal Love.

On the other hand, for his dream to come true, he could choose another world. One of unbelievable sacrifice, a deep, dark hole in his life without his love during more than a year of total isolation and emotional death. To some this time apart may appear as a mere blink of the eye compared to a lifetime, but for a young couple in love it would be an eternity. Wayne, with his double-edged sword of Free Will, is the only one who can choose this path of loneliness if their future of love together is to ever be.

Wayne searches for true employment for the entire 90-day decision window, but fails. Caught in the middle of the decision of his destiny, Wayne soon learns the military is again battling his enemy, Russia. Threats and fear of another War are everywhere, but this time it is the terror of a world nuclear holocaust. It is now a world void of even the simplest of joys and dreams, and a world of unbelievable struggles to survive.

Yet, it is a battle Wayne knows he must join, not only to earn his and Annie's miracle pot of gold, but because he has a lasting sense of duty to his country, in spite of the violent death all around him. He still hopes he can help forge a better world without War, which he believes could be done, if he could only discover its dark secrets.

The time for decision has ended. His impossible choice is now cast, not just in stone, but possibly in his very blood. If he survives his frozen Alaskan Hell and the battles with his personal Demons, Fears and Wild Beasts, Wayne may just discover his true destiny, one he cannot yet comprehend. It may not be one of just destroying his poverty and the guilt of George's death, but a destiny he *must* survive to fulfill, the ultimate call to sacrifice his life to save his country, his friends and all those he loves.

Just before noon, on the 90th day, Wayne reports to a little-known hotel, walks down a dimly lit hall, and pauses at a door with no number. Turning back is no longer possible for him. A knock on the door, a pause of seemly hours, and then a sterile, bland voice almost whispers, "Enter."

Wayne opens the rusty-hinged door and steps into a one-light-bulb room, blinds down, to squint at a plain-suited man behind a small table. The man points to a folding chair and slides a document to Wayne. At the end is a place for three signatures, dates and, strangely, even time.

The suited man asks Wayne, "Do you need to read it again?"

Wayne hesitates and answers, "It makes no difference now."

The suited man then points to an X. Wayne assumes that's where he is supposed to sign his name, and he does so. Before he has a chance to write in the date, the suited man takes the document, dates it, and looks at his watch and pauses. They both sit in silence. Wayne looks at his watch. Two minutes to 12 noon. He must have arrived a little early for his meeting. More silence, then the suited man glances one more time at his watch, and writes in the date and time by Wayne's name. Precisely 12 noon.

He then picks up the agreement, signs it just out of Wayne's view, and puts it in his brief case, saying, "You'll receive further instructions," and points to the door.

As Wayne departs for home, he wonders, *Why was there a third signature line? Who will sign it, and when?*

The Last Dance

This is our final night together, a night of ultimate choice. It is our last dance before separation for yet another young lover's eternity.

The dark and gloom all around us blanket our hearts and souls on this last night together, waiting for our uncertain tomorrow. It is not at all as it was on that starlit night with the golden moon when we first met and danced so close, two fateful years ago. But on this night, just minutes ahead, down a lonely narrow road deep in the woods next to a gentle, winding stream, rests a little cabin impatiently waiting for us. It, too, knows it's our last time together, our last dance, soon to be apart for yet another eternity. With distant memories and thoughts of first love beyond human words, our journey together here will all too quickly come to an end.

The door secure, the tiny candle lit. Oh, to have the full joy of this last dance, this last caress, and relive the gentle fragrance of her special perfume, the soft music of love. Yet, once again, we must battle the human passions of long-delayed love. I feel it is not fair. But, as I was forced to learn through my best friend's violent death, life is not fair. Fairness is not given, but as with all things of value, must be earned through the struggles of life and, sometimes, even death.

The journey soon before me may just open the long-sealed doors to such mysteries of life, but for now I must believe all things happen for some reason I do not yet understand. Fair or not, Annie and I still wish for our dream of true Eternal Love to finally come true in this place, at this time. Yet, not by divine guidance or rule from above, but by our God-given Free Wills, we have once again chosen to keep within ourselves all the joys and fulfillment of a true marriage until my return from Arctic Hell, a journey to the unknown of frigid darkness beginning, not next year, next month, or even next week, but tomorrow.

Hours together become just an instant. The fragile light of our tiny candle flickers one last time and dies, as did the lives of those other young lovers with their own forbidden dream of eternal love, Romeo and Juliet. When our waiting apart is finally over, we pray our new world will not be one of Disaster and Death as theirs was, but one of life and love. Back into this dark and gloomy night we go, void of any joy, remembering the last dance that never was. With one last kiss, and holding trembling hands, we travel back to our own separate homes, our own separate lives, our own separate worlds, for yet another eternity apart, leaving as we came—in silence.

Separation Sadness

Another eternity of separation is thrust upon our young lives. Annie and I are at a Chicago airport saying goodbye, once again, for almost a year and a half apart. My new life of discovery and survival begins on this May 5th, exactly two years since my Annie and I first met. We are now silently sitting, holding hands, in a distant Chicago airport, nervously waiting for me to be taken on my impossible journey into the frightening Arctic world. Yes, taken to that place were even God would never want to go. A place where, if He ever chose to give the world a long-overdue flushing, that's where He would do it. It's a perpetually freezing and desolate world of total human isolation, the Arctic. Yet I am not going to this frightening world by any demand or commandment from above, but by my own Free Will.

I truly believe that no matter what new challenges I must face during these journeys into my new, frightening worlds of fears, hideous beasts and countless enemies, I must survive at all costs. I have a powerful reason, for sitting next to me in this nearly empty airport is my Eternal Love. She is struggling to put on an encouraging smile just for me.

I know she is more than a little upset about my asking, "Will you marry me?" and then saying, "I'll see you again in about a year or so. I won't blame you if you leave me for a sane man while I am away playing with the beasts of the Arctic."

She must really love me, though, because here she is, in this cold and damp airport, holding me and whispering, "Goodbye," and, "Come back to me safe."

All too soon, the final call for me to get on board this huge plane with four gigantic engines painfully shouts in my ears.

"I'll see you later, Honey. I'll come back to you in one piece, Annie, and chocked full of love." Now, that sounds rather stupid, but I really mean it. She then gives me one last parting hug and kiss. That's a truly courageous lady for you.

Through the departure gate, up the boarding stairs, and finally in my assigned seat on this plane to our destiny of delayed love. As it begins to roll down the runway, I struggle not to shout for it to stop and return me to a normal life with my love. No, it must go on, for we have made our heartbreaking decision together. We have already been two years apart while separated by the army. Yet, once again, it's a lonely voyage to the unknown away from our love, for a very, very long time.

The rumbling of the plane's tires against the pavement pounds in my ears, then quiets, and we are at last in the air. Like it or not, this agonizing journey to the Alaskan Arctic begins. I know not when and where I will be thousands of miles from home. All I know right now is that for a very long time I will no longer see my

Annie and my Chicago, with its chaotic Midway airport, its spaghetti-like expressways and its majestic skyline, for they are dissolving into the darkening clouds of a possible Midwestern thunderstorm. I wonder if this is some kind of sign, warning the pilot to turn this plane around and make a safe landing while he still can, and a quick return to my lovely lady. But there is no turning around. No landing. No welcome back home hug for me, for now.

I wave goodbye one last time, knowing Annie cannot possibly see me. As I finish my feeble wave, I notice the stewardess giving me this crazy look, as if I have just escaped from an insane asylum. I think that's where I should be about now, but I guess I'm stuck with my impulsive decision to make this ridiculous trip north to Alaska. I have many reasons for taking this journey into Arctic Hell, but right now I can't remember even one good one, except Annie. Yet, in my heart, I feel Annie

returning my final overwhelming wave of sadness, for she, too, is alone once more, praying that our Impossible Dream of a better world will come true.

All alone now, at this cold and damp airport, once again without my beloved Wayne. I struggle to wave one last time at you, my Soldier Boy, yet I know you cannot see me any longer. The next time we are together will be in over a year. I cannot hold back my tears as I silently wait at this lonely airport for a ride back home.

It will not be the fancy wedding limo we had hoped for by this time. No, just a bus that will take me back to Whiting, Indiana. Even though I will be surrounded by many happy travelers, I know it will be a very long, sad journey for me. I cannot think now about what kind of uncertain, even terrible, life you will soon live in the far

44

Arctic of Alaska. But I know my life will also be totally different than when we first met.

There have been hard times in our struggles to know and understand each other since then, especially during your early army career, but I believe that these are all part of a deeper love growing between us. Our love is tested even more as I silently sit holding my once beautiful handkerchief, now limp from my many tears. I know that you had no choice but to leave me here, far behind.

I also know, through all your many struggles yet to come, you are dedicated to do the very best job you can, no matter where you must go. We are both determined to save all the money we can while you are away. Precious funds we desperately need for our wonderful dream of some distant tomorrow, of long-awaited marriage, a family, and college.

While we wait and work until then, we are determined to survive together, no matter what comes our way. Even though our bodies will be thousands of miles apart, through my unconditional love for you, I know we will be joined together by our hearts and souls, even in the darkest of times. Because, when you love someone and believe in him as I do in you, you can do anything to make an impossible dream come true. Oh, I so dream of flying to you right now, my Soldier Boy...right now.

David is Born

Wayne and Annie's last loving kiss at the airport quickly becomes only a cherished memory. After exactly two years of separation since they first met, their desperate journey for forbidden love begins again, May 5, 1959.

For one year and three months—455 endless days—of constant loneliness, they will be apart once more while Wayne battles a frozen Arctic Hell to earn Annie's love and discover the secrets of War.

This dreaded journey apart from my love begins with my flight of thousands of miles over high mountains, winding rivers, and frozen lands dead of any life-giving green.

The fear of the unknown world ahead forces me to realize I can no longer bear the agonizing sound of

George calling out for "Wayne" to save him from his slaughter. The time of decision I have rejected for so long is now forced upon me. In an attempt to create a new life, and put my fears and guilt of my past behind me, I am finally driven to change my name. That frightful name must be buried deep in my soul until I find redemption and freedom from the guilt of George's murder, when I may deserve his heavenly friendship once again.

To mask the shame and guilt of letting my best friend violently die, I must change my name. From now on, my new family will only know me by my middle name, "David." As with the first David from the distant past who slay the giant, as this new David, I am also now left alone to battle my own Goliath of Death and Slaughter to try to survive in this new world of Frozen Terror and War.

In spite of my never-ending fear of dying at War, to save all I love, I have no other choice but to stop Global

Nuclear War. To complete this impossible mission, I pray I have just one fragment of my best friend's boundless courage. This is no longer a vow of just wishful intent that I created in reaction to George's violent death, but now it's a vow I fully believe. That just one person *can* help create a new world without War...even if only for one day.

Choice and Swords

"Oh, Michael, my spiritual father, you are the only father I have ever known. As never before, I must desperately seek out your infinite wisdom. Once I believed in you and in your power to heal, forgive and guide searching travelers in life. Do you not hear my cries for help, as it was from that other man of doubting faith, also torn apart by fear and grief? His call of agony still echoes from over 2,000 years ago, "Why have you forsaken me?"

"David, you called? We are here with you, in your mind, heart, and soul. Believe in us once again."

"Michael, what about George?"

"David, your friend in life is now with us in death, but with eternal life. He knows of all the countless struggles before you in your many tomorrows of confusion and pain. The time to search for deliverance from your perpetual life of fear, doubt, and guilt is before you.

Yet, true deliverance it is not a gift without trials. All the graces in life must be earned, or they have little value in guiding you along your struggles for wisdom. Yes, David, all those who love you now and in the past will always be with you in spirit. They will come to help guide you on your journey, the path for knowledge and understanding of your troubled life. Your aids they will be but, with your gift of Free Will, you must choose."

"How do I choose the right path? I'm afraid. I do not have the boundless courage that once lived in my friend George. My world of today is a web of confusion and darkness."

"David, beware of the glitter of wealth, and search for the wisdom to understand War, for which you seek to earn love. For it is the power of a strong mind that fully opens the path to the light within you. This light is the path to the truth and the riches of the universe. Believe that yet to be born is the boundless courage and wisdom for which you seek. Search well for the truth, for it is hidden deep within the darkness of your fear and guilt. It is only the truth that will set you free. Trust in the light, your growing love, and your hidden mental talents. These are your swords in the many battles against WAR that is yet to come. All the paths you take for good or for evil in search of the truth must be your choice, and only your choice. Choose wisely, my son. Choose wisely."

"To save the very lives and souls of all I love, I vow that while on this journey to my salvation, I will find the truth about this plague on humankind called War and discover the secrets that can destroy it from within."

I suddenly jerk awake from my bewildering dream. Or was it an endless nightmare? We climb higher and higher, until we are on top of those clouds by at least a couple of miles. I don't know how high this plane flies, but I know the up and down pressure changes make my ears clog up and then pop. Sometimes it even hurts a little, but chewing gum helps my ears clear up faster.

Even though this is a very fast four-engine airplane, the trip already seems extremely long. I have been told that these four-engine planes can fly, for a while at least, with only two engines working. I hope we don't have to find out the hard way if this is really true. Even though I am afraid of heights, I try not to worry about the engines anymore.

At last the Rocky Mountains come up just ahead, on my right side. It makes me feel very insignificant when I realize how high the mountains must be, compared to how small they appear at our altitude. How tiny my current problems and concerns must be when compared to those in the rest of the world, even in Alaska. On my left, I can see the gambling capital of Las Vegas on the distant horizon and can just imagine all the money foolishly floating around down there as it's spent on needless luxuries.

Yet, here I am, going to unknown worlds of anxiety and fear to make just enough extra money to get married and hopefully have a moderate life with Annie. *Well, whoever said life is fair? Certainly not me.* Enough of this philosophical talk. Aside from the humming of the four engines, which the pilot never quite got to totally work together without that whirring sound, the trip has been pretty uneventful.

Once again I am thankful for my four turning engines, with their humming of a special tune just for me, a lullaby soothing a weary traveler to sleep. As the sun begins to set and night takes over the sky, I wonder just how many sunrises and sunsets I will soon never see as I enter this land of eternal winter. In this northernmost desolate land, the sun almost never shines for over 10 months out of the year. Once again, I begin to doubt the wisdom of making this journey into what might just be the frozen Arctic Hell of my death. For better or worse I try to suppress thoughts about my uncertain future. With a long flight still ahead, I might as well look a little deeper into that contract I signed, especially some of that fine print nobody ever reads.

Bloody Agreement

"The Government will withhold all the funds you earn until your contract has been successfully completed, precisely at 12 noon, on your very last day of your agreement. Your emotional or physical hardships, even your death, will not alter this agreement. If you survive the Arctic, but fail in your mission in any way, the funds held for you will be forfeited and you must leave as you came."

If David fails, returning with just the clothes of poverty on his back, he will forever live with the guilt of causing the death of his and Annie's Impossible Dream of a life of Lasting Peace and Eternal Love.

David is overwhelmed by the sudden regret of his fateful decision to make this traumatic journey. As much as he struggles to reject him, the demon in David's mind, WAR, once again overcomes his senses.

"Well, David, you did it. Deserting all you love again for the riches of the world. How selfish can you get? Oh, now come the regrets. Poor little David."

"Oh, go back into that deep, dark hole of fear in my mind. I just wish I had some idea what I'm really getting into."

"Wish granted, Davy boy. Wish granted!"

"What do you mean, 'wish granted?'"

WAR knows that many times he will have to battle all the forces he hates, the very ones David brings with him to the Arctic—his Free Will, Friendships and, above all, his Love. Fear is WAR's greatest weapon against him.

"David, I warn you. I will discover your strengths, weaknesses, fears, and doubts of your courage so I may defeat you in our battles for your mortal soul. Let the trials begin."

Fantasy Journey

"Behold your world of doom!" WAR thunders.

"You are not real, just another vision of my tortured past."

"True, David. Oh, so true. Enjoy!"

"Go to HELL!"

"Later, David, later. Maybe next time—for *real*! Do you believe it, David? We have just flown thousands of miles in no time, literally, on my Black Magic watch. Let me show you where we are in a way even a dumb human being like you can understand.

"Since I know you are afraid of heights and flying, I thought we would start our vacation here with a little crash landing. It really hasn't happened–yet. But you *are* sitting on the tip of the nose of a White Polar Bear, perched on the edge of the Arctic Ocean. This nose is actually the tip of a mile-high mountain that looks just like a very large, life-threatening Polar Bear Head, when seen from 8,000 feet. It's the home of a top-secret government radar site manned by 150 air force "volunteers" and a few insane civilians, like you, David. You realize, of course, it could be bombed by your enemy at any moment, if I want.

"The very cold and very deep Arctic Ocean far below you is unbelievably dark blue. In fact, it's almost black, and very cold compared to the warm, gray water of the Bering Strait. Where these two bodies meet, they battle each other to survive, and the violent weather they create becomes totally unpredictable and dangerous. The pungent and nauseating smell of rotting giant animal carcasses slowly drifts up this barren mountain. You can hear the scream of wild beasts battling each other to the death for the last piece of winter food, or a prized mate. In the still of a bitter cold night, you can hear the thunderous sound of giant slabs of Arctic ice violently slamming into the fragile beach and your little shack of survival. Your only home is slowly losing warmth. With your shelter gone, this hurricane wind will freeze young skin in less than 30 seconds. You must now struggle to try to survive until the very end, when you finally must battle the Demon of Death, *me*, your personal War."

I suddenly feel the concussion and thunder of Russian bombs. Has the time of world annihilation finally come?

I jerk back to reality and soon realize it's not the sound of invasion, but the rumble of the landing gears being lowered and the not-so-gentle bouncing onto the runway at last. I must finally be at my first stop along these thousands of miles to my awaiting Frozen Hell. Was this my future, only written in my confused mind? Was it a vision of what must be my fate, something my Faith and Free Will may alter, or is this the foreshadowing of the countless chapters that can be or must be written of my life, or even death?

What's Next

As we taxi to the terminal, the stewardess tells me my luggage is being transported to my next aircraft. I wonder, *What will my Arctic lifeline be? A big plane, small plane, or a dog sled?* I climb on board my next plane, which will take me in only one direction. North.

With a strange look in her eyes, the stewardess looks at me and asks, "Are you sure you still want to take this journey of your young life forever North?"

What a strange thing for a person with her professional training to say to a passenger. It's as if she is trying to frighten me out of taking this flight. Or am I just imagining it from the dark side of my mind?

Now, I have just been told my next plane seems to have developed an engine noise and we need to return to the Seattle airport for repairs. After a successful landing and a very long break, I'm told the plane will take longer than expected to repair. This same stewardess tells us there is another plane, a not-as-roomy-and-quiet military aircraft, available. She also tells us there are two important air force bases near Anchorage, and some military personnel are on board who are expected to be there this evening. I am also expected to be picked up at the airport tonight so that I may report for my first day of training tomorrow morning. By her anxious speech I believe her home base is also Anchorage, and after a long cross-country flight she, too, would like to get home tonight. With no other choice, with all the other stranded passengers, I drag myself to whatever flying object will take me forever North, again and again.

A "not-as-roomy-and-quiet military aircraft" is an understatement. It has only two engines, and it is the same olive drab color as that old army uniform I am so desperately trying to forget.

Fire, Fire

My seat belt is fastened, my barf bag is handy, my deodorant is actively fighting my sweat, and all those instructions about seat belts and emergency oxygen are completed. The plane begins to roll, and roll, and roll. Then lift off, and the rumbling noise stops, until two loud thumps (wheels coming up, I hope). Hurrah, finally up in the Wild Blue Yonder.

My plane goes higher and higher into the air, and no head or stomach problems, yet. Both engines on this very old Army plane seem to be purring fine (at least I think so) and all appears to be well. The seat belt light goes off and everybody unbuckles theirs. I can do the same...uh, on second thought, maybe not. But at least I do put my barf bag away.

I am really lucky to get a large window seat (yeah, lucky). Getting up enough courage to actually look outside, I follow along the wing and expect to see the end of it disappear into the black of night. Instead, I am shocked to see, of all things, the engine is not only glowing red and white, but is actually belching fire like a medieval dragon! *What about the other engine, the one I can't see?*

My deodorant is now on major overload and my barf bag ready for a quick redraw. In panic mode, now, I call the stewardess over and point out this possible little problem with, at least this engine—maybe both—being on fire.

She smiles, and whispers in my ear, "That's normal, sir. Coffee, tea or Coke?"

This young lady is very calming, but may be lacking a little knowledge about burning airplanes. She is also probably very attractive—but I have another very important issue on my mind just now, like survival, and why did she question me about my flying on these planes taking me forever North?

I try to believe what she just told me is meant to be comforting and that I should finally relax. But I continue to see my engine burning even brighter as the night becomes more of a deep black hole in the sky. *Is there a giant explosion yet to come? If so, will I just be one of the glowing little pieces left over from the "Big Bang," fluttering back down to earth along with parts of propellers and even that blankety-blank engine that caused all this trouble to start with? Where would I land, in some farmer's pig pen, or worse?*

Enough is enough with all these "maybes" and "what ifs." I try to put all these fears of dismal possibilities in the back of my brain with all my other both real and imagined fears and move on to gradually start believing all this "normal engine burning" stuff. Fear has a way of playing games with time, and before I realize it my flight soon ends with a safe and happy landing. It's now the thump of those wheels finally coming back down, and those beautiful Anchorage airport buildings and other parked planes and trucks coming up to meet me.

Hurrah!

I have been a true survivor once again. Yes, a survivor, not so much in the actual physical sense, because there was no real engine fire, but in a very emotional way. I conquered some of my fears of flying, fought the battle of my mind, and I won. Or did I? I soon realize I cannot yet imagine the battles I must fight to survive in the eternity of months before me.

Beginning this first night away from all that I know and understand, with all I love so far behind.

Arctic Training

My new home is at a secret location outside Elmendorf Air Force Base, Anchorage, Alaska. Here, I will be trained in the operation and maintenance of the top secret radio equipment used to guard the entire coast of Alaska from Russian attack. The schedule is grueling during the week. On weekends I am free, and even expected, to explore the far north world around me, when accompanied by my fellow students and instructor, for security reasons.

Since the information I am taught is classified, I am told not to disclose anything dealing with the project to others, including Annie. This puts a strain on our ability to be honest with each other, but our trust and love holds firm.

The special radio communication systems I was trained to use in the military are very similar to what I am now being taught. This is very helpful during training, but later causes me to wonder if being first in the class is always the best.

Upon graduation from the training, I believe my good grades will earn me the best site on the southern Alaskan coast, Anchorage. Then, Annie could come up and we could build a good life during my next 12 months of duty.

Instead, with my broader knowledge of all aspects of the equipment, I am assigned to the communications site that's most critical to protect. It's also the coldest, darkest, most dangerous, and most isolated location in Alaska, the northern beach of the Arctic Ocean. It's the first point of any enemy invasion from Russia over the North Pole. It is so secret, isolated, and dangerous that civilians, especially wives, are not allowed. It's certainly not a home for my Annie.

At first I am very disappointed. Then, I realize I was picked because there was a need to have the most technically experienced persons at this most critical site. I figure I should be proud of that and accept the mission to go to the Arctic, vowing to do the best job I can. As hard as it is to be even further away from her, I know Annie will also be proud of my decision.

One of the greatest honors I have during this time is meeting and talking with one of the most honored inventors of the 20th Century. In his younger days, he was the assistant to the man who invented television. He became the inventor of the system that saved so many lives and helped defeat the enemy during World War Two, radar.

He also invented the same technology that I learned and was taught in the military, microwave radio. He is visiting our training center on an inspection tour because it is those same technologies of radar and high-power microwave that are used to transmit the radio signals from site to site within the Alaska National

Defense system. After reviewing the background of all the students, he asks to speak with the person with the most experience and knowledge of some of the equipment he helped invent. The school director introduces him to me.

As we talk, he describes in detail the inner workings of this transmitter tube he named a "Klystron." I believe his only regret might be the extra heat and dangerous microwave radiation they generate, which requires a liquid cooling system and a shielded cabinet. He says he believes people will some day cook with this same microwave radio energy, but with far less power and danger than the transmitters I must use.

For many reasons, I will forever remember our talk together, especially the details about the heat and radiation problems, and I am inspired by his passion to be an inventor like him. The world lost a great and caring man just weeks after we spoke at the training center. His name? Doctor Russell Varian.

Exploring

Once we all have our additional security clearances, we can start exploring the wonders of the Arctic together.

We meet the family of four choosing to live off the land and lakes in the wilderness, far from civilization and the threats of another War. We also inquire about the colorful little houses outside a tiny village, built by the native tribes to house the bodies and souls of their departed because burial in the soft tundra ground is impossible. Our most enjoyable times are the weekend volleyball games with my new friends, especially Peggy, Frank, and Sue. We occasionally have outside dinners under the stars to think about our new world of isolation.

Most important of all is the package every month from Annie. The slightly torn brown paper is covered in beautiful art and ribbons outside. Inside, it contains the most delicious fudge I've ever had and a bundle of love letters. The fudge I share with my friends. The letters I selfishly keep to myself for those midnight hours when I have trouble sleeping.

Forbidden Love

The final two days of David's three months of training, Sue receives glorious news. The next day will be her first as a trained stewardess for Alaska Airlines, but when Sue hears that David is not going to spend the next full year at Anchorage, but at the worst, most dangerous site on the Arctic Ocean, she keeps her joyful news to herself and searches out David. Burying her true feelings about David deep in her heart and soul, she tells him he trained himself to become the very best, and he is, so he must go where he is being sent. All his instructors determined only he has all the knowledge and experience needed to keep the most critical Arctic location alive in case of a major emergency.

That night, all of the friends David has trained with for three months also find out where they have been assigned. His closest friend, Frank, is stationed at Kotzebue, the next site south of the Cape where David will be. The others are scattered all along the Alaskan coast. A member from another team training with David was awarded Anchorage.

With all the assignments—both happy and sad—disclosed, Sue can no longer keep her good news to herself and tells everyone about her first flight as a stewardess the next day. Peggy's mother announces a dinner she has planned for the next night to honor Sue's big day, and as a going away party for all those leaving for their assigned sites the day after.

The next evening, when Sue's first flight lands, Peggy, Frank, and I are there to greet her. As Sue leaves her plane, she sees us waiting and runs towards us happily laughing. Sue jumps into my arms with an unexpected hug and holds me tight against her chest.

She wants me to feel I should no longer think of her as a teenage volleyball player and a young girl of just 19. Instead, she soon will be 20. It is now time for me to realize that, in just three short months, she has become a mature woman, in every way. She then takes my hand one last time.

The party that night is a great success with many stories of the hard training, the fun side trips, and showing off fur parkas that some have saved up their money to buy. After handshakes, hugs, and sad parting words, the next year of adventures, struggles, and fears of the unknown begin for all who have had the courage to come to the last frontier, Alaska.

The following morning begins the most fearful journey of my still young life. My good friends Peggy, Frank, and Sue are at the airport to see me off on my first of more flights even further North. I say a sad farewell and board my first small bush plane.

Knowing he can no longer hear her, shaking with grief, Sue sends a message from her aching heart to her

Forbidden Love.

David, last night, after leaving my plane, I just had to run to you and jump into your arms. It was the one and only time you let me hold you so very close. You will never know how much our simple friendship has grown since our first volleyball game.

When you discovered that I must live the life of a military child, always moving from base to base, never knowing a school or friend for more than a year, you became a close friend. You listened without judging me and my strange ways. With nothing more than a held hand, our talks helped me overcome my troubled family life, and to move on.

But you must forget me now. After your year of duty in the Arctic, you must go back to your long-awaited true love, Annie. I pray you have a wonderful life together. I know I will never see you again, but I can never forget you. You must never know how much I love you.

As David's plane begins to roll, he looks out the window one more time, searching for remembered joy, but instead sees Peggy and Frank hugging his friend Sue as she cries. David's mostly bright adventures in Anchorage are now tainted with the dark sadness of Sue's departing tears. He prays she will find the true love and happiness for which she has so desperately searched.

Ever Northward

As the overpowering fear of the unknown saturates my struggling mind, I fight to suppress agonizing visions of the sights, sounds, and smells of a world doomed to catastrophe if I fail in my mission to protect all I love from our enemy. Visions of the stupidity of Global Nuclear War and its violent ending explode in my ever-weakening mind.

High in the heavens looms the gift of the giant mushroom grown in the polluted soil of greed, selfishness, and stupidity of all mankind. As real as life and death itself, my eyes feel the burn of the world I love dissolving in a pool of boiling blood. Only the strongest concrete structures are left standing, though they are just empty shells, raped of anything inside, as they are engulfed by 4,000-degree flames, devouring both man and machine.

The Hurricane Winds and the roar of death subside,

and I am overcome by deafening silence. No cries for help. No screams of agonizing pain from burning throats. No stench of rotting bodies or even burning flesh for, at this temperature, even the remaining bones are instantly disintegrated. The fine dust of loved ones alive just seconds before, now cremated, blocks out the sun and permeates each breath I struggle to salvage.

Yes, these dead are the lucky ones. It's the poor souls who survive just a few miles beyond ground zero who suffer the most. Burnt flesh rolls off their naked bodies like sheets of spring rain off a newly-cleaned window. They will soon die a painful, agonizing death. Still further from the center of Hell, others feel the patterns of their clothing fused into their backs, arms, and disfigured faces. They pray for the gift of death, but it may not come tomorrow, next week, or even next year, but it will truly come as the insides of their human form decomposes, eaten away by the plague of Radiation Poisoning. Have all those who are to die now left this earth, their voices never to be heard again, or is it the destruction of my eardrums blown apart by the concussion bellowing from this giant mushroom of human folly?

In my bones I feel the voices of those once great leaders shout to the heavens, "Oh, GOD, I pray that we could go back in time and stop this Terrible Nuclear Holocaust before it ever started!"

I believe only our own decisions can determine our yet-to-be-written future. Once again, I hear my mother's words of wisdom, spoken to me after having survived the global horror of World War Two. "Those Who Ignore History Are Doomed to Repeat It," Edmund Burke (1729-1797).

I jerk awake from these nightmares. This time, they do not come from my dark past, but are visions of a possible tomorrow for all I love due to my failures. I pull from my subconscious mind the vow I made to George so many thousands of miles and months before.

In spite of my never ending fear of dying at War, to save all I love, I have no other choice but to become an Arctic Secret Agent, battling Lies, Spies, and Wild Beasts to discover the secret to stop Global Nuclear War. To complete this impossible mission, I pray I have one small fragment of my friend's boundless courage.

This is the third time David has repeated his vow to George and all he loves. Yet this time, by lot or by fate, it is a vow of determination and action. He has been chosen to possibly be the right person, at the right place, at the right time for a secret security mission into Arctic Hell. His impossible vow to learn the secrets to stop WAR might just come true.

David tries to believe he has a special reason to exist, but for the moment he must settle for seeking the answer in his visions of the future.

Nome Tour

On the way to Nome, expectations of what I'll see for the next year flash before my eyes. Looking out the window, I already see that just a few miles ahead the trees become fewer and fewer. I'm leaving the land of green and grass in August, and going up to the northernmost Arctic, which even now is getting a dusting of snow and winter wind.

The journey is pretty straightforward. I'm in a decent plane with at least a couple of engines and some kind of heater. Will I transfer to something even smaller at the next stop? I don't know quite yet, but I try to think about happy things. What will happen when I get back to the joy of seeing my Annie again—the family, college, children, a job, and not having to go to this godforsaken place just to afford a marriage license?

The journey is relatively quick. I see we are in a town that doesn't look anything like a small town in my area of Hammond, Indiana. We approach the runway. The plane sets down fairly quickly, then we roll off to the side and stop.

Hopping out of the plane and greeting the pilot I met when we first got on, I ask, "How long do you think we're going to be here?"

"Oh, probably a couple of hours. We have to unload some merchandise and then pick up some skins and things from the Eskimos here. Why don't you take a little tour? There's plenty of time and you may meet some interesting people."

"Okay, I'll do that. Thanks."

After a short walk I reach what must be the main part of Nome, just a small town. I see some rather strange things along the side of the road. Cars from about 1957 or 1959, which are not much different from my own back home. But then I notice the wooden sidewalks. It looks more like a town out of a Wild West movie, with little false-front buildings. Not much of any road at all, just kind of compacted dirt, and no hard concrete or asphalt. The town looks rather primitive. As I look down the street I see the strange sides of hoses, spigots, and valves running across the wooden walkways. Nothing seems solid. It just wants to move. I'm interested to talk to someone about all of this. There are small buildings up ahead. There are all kinds of attached buildings with their doors open, as it is August and still fairly warm. I walk into one that's much like any small country store in Georgia, Alabama, or Tennessee. The small stove in the middle of the room is old enough for Ben Franklin to have built it himself. As I look around I see an elderly woman, and I walk up to her.

"It's a very interesting little store you have here. May I look around and maybe take a little tour around Nome?" I ask politely. "I'm on the flight going up to the next level, Kotzebue, and then I guess I'm going to go up further north to a place called The Cape."

She kind of smiles and says, "Oh, it is going to be pretty cold up there," in English not much different from my own.

"Do you mind if I walk around town? Is there anybody who could show me around?"

"Oh, yes, my husband. His name is Nanook."

"Where is he?"

The next thing I know I hear this sort of deep, masculine powerful voice saying, "Right behind you."

"Whoa, where did you come from? I didn't hear you."

"I'm just a quiet one when I walk. You have to be quiet around here when you're sneaking up on Polar Bears, Caribou and other wild animals."

That really disturbs me, but I don't want to show it.

"Of course, I understand, Nanook. But, hopefully, I won't be running into them and have to sneak up behind a Polar Bear or Caribou." I remember a Caribou is sort of like a big burly second cousin to a reindeer, but a lot meaner.

84

"If you're not busy, can you show me a little of your town, Nome?" I ask. "But, I've got less than a couple of hours."

"Sure, I'd like to do that for you. Do you want to look at my wife's store here a bit before we go?"

"Yes, I'd love to."

I begin to chat with Nanook's wife and admire the many tourist trinkets. I can't really pronounce her Eskimo name but, for some reason, I'll never forget Nanook.

She then asks, "What are you going to do after you get back?"

"Well, I'll be up there about a year."

To make me a little more comfortable about my life-to-be up at the Cape, she adds, "Oh, it won't seem that long. What then?"

"When I get back I have a fiancé waiting for me, I hope, and we will be married. Hopefully, I will go back to school, have a family, and get a good job."

"That really sounds like a great goal in life for a young man like you. You said you're going to get married?"

"Yes. We've been waiting already two years plus a number of months while I was in the service."

"Why don't you take the tour with Nanook, and when you get back I'll have a little something for you and your future wife to remember your time up here in the Arctic. You go with Nanook, now, and look around our little town."

"Thank you."

Nanook and I walk out the door and I mention the hoses running around wooden sidewalks, "Why the funny sidewalks, Nanook?"

He replies, "You know that we're sitting on permafrost. Nothing is very solid and it's just like spongy ground floating around on water. You have a thin layer of water and then you have ice. If you try to put anything into the ground, then the permafrost is going to freeze and thaw and freeze again, causing a lot of stress on any pipes and eventually breaking them. We can't really bury much of anything, so we must move with Mother Nature. We move when she moves and our buildings and our sidewalks just kind of float along with her. We tie them pretty well together so that they float. Almost the whole town will float back and forth, so we don't dig into the ground much."

"Nanook, I noticed while flying in that there appears to be a small graveyard or something at some distance from the town."

"Same reason as the houses. We can't bury the bodies because they get pushed back up again. After a while, of course, our dead start to disappear and there's a bad smell. We just sort of put their remains away from the town. We are still close enough to visit. We just put them in their own little area so we don't bother them and they don't bother us."

I think it's really very intriguing. I had heard a similar thing about New Orleans, where the ground is at water level, so they can't really bury anybody in the ground. They put them in vaults, and they last about a year. Then they clear what's left of the remains and use them again for other people. It makes perfect sense to me. As we are walking down the main street, I ask about the cars.

"I notice the cars here are not much different than our cars back home, about 1959 or 1960 models."

Nanook explains, "We do have some fairly well-off people here in town, but most people don't really need cars. We just walk. There's a few old ones here and there, but it takes a lot of money to have cars shipped up here. There are no roads between Anchorage, Fairbanks, and Nome, so they have to come by boat. When the ice of the Bering Strait freezes over, boats cannot come up here until summer comes again."

"That makes sense. So, the cars must be a lot more expensive."

As we walk further down the main street I notice that the streets, too, aren't solid. There is no concrete. There is no asphalt.

Nanook tells me, "It's the same reason we can't bury our dead. We have to roll with Mother Nature and nothing here can be solid. The streets just move along with the permafrost. We just kind of dust off the roads and maybe occasionally put some oil down or something. We can't put anything solid like cement. By the way, if you look across the street there, you'll see a building that looks almost new. It was supposed to be our new post office."

"Why does it have barriers and yellow signs and trash around it?"

"Well, there was some bright young man from the South 48. He came up and was going to beat Mother

Nature. He tried to use very thick cement basement walls and big metal bars. They dug deep into the permafrost and down into the ice below thinking they'd have a solid foundation. They had about a year's worth of work and use out of the post office. Then things began to go bad."

"What happened?"

"It's what you think happened. The permafrost took hold and put a lot of pressure on the foundation. It began to crack and crumble and so the building had to be condemned."

"Two to three years with the forces of nature and the permafrost freezing and thawing must have put a great deal of pressure on the walls."

"Yes, very strong, very strong."

We continue to walk down the street and it looks more and more like an old western town out of the movies. I expect some townspeople to come out and have duels with their six shooters. Occasionally, we run across some children walking down the middle of the street. It looks like they don't really worry about being run over, probably because there aren't many cars.

Then I notice there is a building across the street called Nome Nugget. It must have been some kind of a restaurant, hotel, or even a saloon with ladies of the night. I continue to walk and talk with Nanook as he describes various scenes.

There's a small house, and on it is a partly torn flag of the territory of Alaska. Alaska just become the 49th state in May of this year, and they probably don't have a new 49-star flag, or may not be able to afford it. I believe they're still very much proud of their new state.

After more turns and a few additional sites, Nanook tells me it's getting late so we better turn around. On the way back I look over at an interesting shack. It almost looks like part of a railroad boxcar. It's painted red and there's a sign on it.

"Yes, we have people, now and in the past, who have come up and lived in it writing books," Nanook tells me. "It's one of the cabins that Rex Beach isolated himself in and wrote some of his books about the gold rush times. There were other authors who came up and wrote their books about the north and its dogs, like Jack London and his *Call of the Wild.*

"We've had a number of people who have come up and just walked around. They may just want to think about what it was like in the old days of gold fever, about a hundred years ago. It started in the Yukon and then came over to Nome. Nome got a reputation for being a pretty wild town in those days. Now, we are kind of back to normal again, nice and quiet. Except for all the tourists. That's okay, because they're mostly nice, and their money helps us send our kids to school."

As we turn back towards Nanook's wife's store, we see more interesting scenes. I'm almost walking back in time, except for an occasional late 1950s car. We reach the doorway of her little shop. She's smiling and has something wrapped in some old newspaper in her hands.

"I have some presents for you and your future wife," She says as she unwraps the paper. Low and behold, there are little his and hers Eskimo dolls with fur around their hooded heads. I am amazed by the intricacy in the work, especially their little hand-painted faces.

I ask her, "What material is the dolls' hoods?"

She grins, "Oh, that's very precious Wolverine."

"What's Wolverine?"

"It's animal fur with hairs like straws. It's hollow, so it traps warm air. When you breathe in it, it warms up. It's what we use on our parka hoods to keep our faces warm."

Not only do they use Wolverine fur in their own hooded parkas, but even put it on their dolls.

"I'm just so impressed with your fine work. How much do they cost?"

"Oh, it's my present to you and your future wife. So strong to wait so long for you to go back to her. Please, take them back with you and give them to your new wife on your wedding day."

I feel so good about her warm gesture that, even though I'm not sure what the custom is, I hold her hand and, with a small touch, kiss her on the cheek.

She smiles and says, "Have a good life and have lots of babies."

It is very emotional. First, a new life here, and then hopefully a new and wonderful life back with my fiancé, Annie, after a year. But, we have to get through this next year apart and lonely. I turn to thank Nanook for the tour and he says the strangest thing to me.

"We will meet again." I do not know quite what that means. As I look at him bewildered, he smiles, shakes my hand, and says, "Have a good life and remember us."

94

I know that I'll be coming back through Nome in about a year, but I'm not sure if I can stop with enough time to even say hello to my new friends. Turning away, I look at my watch. I better get back to the airplane. I don't want to hold anybody up for any reason.

As I turn around, I hear Nanook saying, "Oh, they'll wait for you. They have to."

Walking back down the road to the waiting plane, I turn around one more time to see them standing in the doorway waving. I wave back and think again about this phenomenal couple. This experience of Nome, the great people I've met, the sights, and even the smells of drying fish, all tell me there's so much more to learn about my new world of the far north. With hundreds of miles yet to travel, ever northward, I'm just beginning to learn the hidden secrets of the Arctic. Yet, I will never forget this small village out of the past, as over the next year of isolation, I struggle to understand my true role in life, my destiny.

Only Two Engines

A short walk and I'm back at the Nome airport. But where is that shiny new plane that brought me here? Instead, parked on the runway, is something that looks like the Wright brothers may have experimented with it in the early 1920s. My pilot tells me, "We had a little engine problem with the plane you came to Nome on, so we had to borrow one from a local bush pilot. He says he has had it since it was new and that he keeps it running himself, so it's perfectly safe to fly. He'll do the flying."

I nervously ask my first pilot, "Do I have any other choice?"

He smiles a little, and jokingly answers, "Not unless you want to take a dog sled, and it's a long way for them to run in all this mushy tundra soil. You can always wait until everything freezes over in a month or two, then they could run faster."

He smiles again, knowing I have no other choice, and tells me, "Your new bush pilot really knows his way around up here. He usually takes tourists hunting Polar Bears to his favorite sites, and has only lost a few who wandered off. He'll get you to wherever you are going just fine."

I tell him, "Thank you for the information–I think."

I am now resigned to my fate, having to believe it will all work out okay–I hope and even pray a little.

It's time to say farewell to Nome, leaving my new friends far behind. I'm just beginning the next leg of my journey to the far Arctic. Once on board, I find this new plane does not have the comforting security of the earlier purr of four engines, or even the two of my military plane three months ago. Instead, I am boarding an ancient three-engine monster with a new, much older, bush pilot—he's at least 45 or 50.

I am so dead tired about now, I really don't care what

engines might already be dead or what they sound like as long as this thing has wings. I will even take a giant albatross, or eagle, or whatever they have in the Arctic that won't eat me and will just get me where I am supposed to go. With the roar—no longer a gentle hum—of this strange airplane's engines, I start to doze off. In this, the even colder wonderland of the Arctic, and in my groggy daze, I say to myself *Well, at least it isn't that Dog Sled—yet.* Time for a little snooze, maybe a big one.

Wow. My little slumber must have been much more than a short nap. I think I am dreaming when the roar of at least one engine, maybe even all three, jerks me awake. It is not the comforting, soothing hum of those many powerful engines that have become part of my travels and provided me some reasonable Arctic comfort. Instead, I begin to hear and even feel the deafening roar of only two engines, if I'm really lucky.

Why is there all this coughing and sputtering? What form of air travel is this? If I get to wherever I'm going, what am I going to live in? Will I have a one- or two-story igloo? What strange creatures will try to room with me?

I'm fully awake now, but still thinking about the weird dreams I just had about my Annie and strange demons and spirits. Many times, dreams can seem so absolutely real. I discover we are about 200 miles above the Arctic Circle, 400 miles from the nearest village and 600 miles north of any kind of road. I soon realize that the roar of the engines is quieter now because one of them, the center one, has a propeller that isn't turning anymore. I look over at our, hopefully, extremely experienced bush pilot, but he appears to be totally unconcerned with our plight.

I can only believe that this engine's quitting is nothing new to him, and has probably happened quite often in its half-century of existence. Maybe it's just like our aging pilot, taking a nap in midflight.

Humor

I try to think of something humorous to shout to the pilot over the remaining two engines' roar, and say, "One down and two to go."

Besides the slight engine problem, I sense that I am slowly going deaf. Could it be because my radio set is old and doesn't have much padding left to filter out most of the engine's noise? I temporarily lift them from my head and feel my eardrums about to burst. Back on they go, very quickly. No matter how bad, I guess something is better than nothing, even if it is 50 years old. I might survive all the wild beasts of the Arctic, but not if I can't hear their threatening growls of pending attack when I finally get there.

The weather is getting rather rough and bouncy right about now and the strong North Arctic wind is starting to make the plane fly backwards. I know that can't be too good on our struggling remaining two engines. Me and my big mouth, tempting fate the way I did. One of the two engines left begins to cough and sputter. Our super-experienced (I hope) pilot plays with the instrument panel controls, probably the throttle or choke, or something like that. He tries to use the radio, but the storm interference is so bad he cannot raise anyone to answer our call for help.

Right now I don't need to examine what he is doing, as long as he gets something to work. While he is playing, I am trying to find some airport. Not likely. Even in this emerging storm I can see there is nothing but miles and miles of this Arctic Tundra. Just soggy weeds and mud, everywhere.

To keep my mind off our impending doom, I try to think of something humorous again, and all I can think of is part of an old poem I was forced to learn in high school. I think it comes from *The Rime of the Ancient Mariner*, "Water, Water Everywhere and Not a Drop to

Drink." Where I am now, it would be more like "Tundra, Tundra Everywhere and Not a Place to Land."

I quickly glance over at my pilot again, only to see him struggling with our dying engine even more while the Tundra below us gets bigger and bigger as we drop further out of the sky. I shut my eyes trying to think of something at least a little more encouraging about our situation. I know it is very bad right now, but I am thankful that I no longer feel the searing heat from that ancient fire-breathing dragon, ready to dive and crash into the unknown below, that I witnessed on my earlier flight. Instead, I am locked in the frigid cold of this half-flying, obsolete aircraft.

I'm also thankful for my miracle pilot, who is still struggling to keep us in the air, though not by much. Suddenly, to my delight, there is no more sputtering and coughing of that second engine. We are back to two running engines again and still have a little air left beneath us. I hope it is enough.

Now, even though I'm still partially deaf, I try to communicate with my pilot. I look over at him, smiling for the first time since we met. I shout to him over our cabin intercom. "Congratulations. You are a miracle worker."

He beams back at me and shouts, "Not me! It's that real miracle worker way up there in the sky who is lifting some of those dark clouds so I can talk on the radio again. Maybe we can find somebody out there who can tell us where we are and how to get where we are supposed to be going."

I look down at that tundra, so close I can smell it. "Do we have enough altitude to keep flying?" I ask.

With my ears almost totally dead by now, I think he answers, "Just," but he might be shouting, "Maybe!"

Flying is just one of the many fears I have developed in my life, fears that come back to haunt me now and then. It is just one of my constant battles against my brain, a sometimes warped mind trying to relive all the traumatic challenges to survive I have had so far in my young life. A strange life, where, for some yet unexplained reason, the demon of Death has passed over me time and time again. I know there must be some reason for my existence. My new life of challenges and battles in this Hell of the North may just start me on my path to understanding who I am and why I still live while others die.

With only two engines left, after many miles on this unbelievable journey, one starts to sputter again, and a winter storm is quickly developing. The pilot tries to call for help, but the signals from his aging radio are too weak to reach their destination. He must search for the Kotzebue village beach with his eyes alone, using dead reckoning and his memories of the flat, soggy tundra he has traveled many times before. With only one good engine and the plane losing altitude and sinking lower and lower, the pilot gets the sputtering engine to run enough to finally reach the beach of Kotzebue. After a safe landing and some temporary repairs, the pilot believes he has fixed the second engine.

Bottoms Up

I can't believe I'm over 6,000 miles from home and only a healthy spit from our Cold War enemy, Russia. Looking again at the one and only escape door, I thank my many flying companions for being with me.

First, there are fresh fruits and vegetables. At least I won't have to worry about dying from sailor's scurvy. Then, I thank my very smelly live chickens. Thank goodness the noise from the engines made me partially deaf hundreds of miles ago and I don't have to join them in their constant clucking conversation. I can't speak their language, anyway. They are probably complaining about how cold it is, not just outside, but inside this ancient airplane.

I'm no aircraft engineer, but I guess if the engines keep quitting like they have, so do the heaters. I am dressed in my fur parka for this near-freezing temperature, but all my chicken companions have only their feathers to flap for a little extra warmth.

Maybe that's why, after many hours of literally flying together, I find myself reading their body language and waving my wings too. I haven't really enjoyed their smell or breathing their feather dust. I guess if eggs keep freezing on their long flights to get up here, you just bring the live chickens along. I know tomorrow at breakfast I will certainly thank them for their country-fresh eggs. My life will be pretty tough up here but theirs will eventually be even worse. Someday, I will meet them again as they become the main course on my dinner table, and I will say a special prayer for my chicken friends.

We are miraculously still up in the air. Not by much, but high enough for me to see our isolated destination on the horizon. Those last few miles are going much too slowly. But, even with coughs and sputters, it looks like our remaining engine may actually get us there, wherever "there" is. As the pilot turns our plane to set up a landing, I see the entire Cape site with its simple attached buildings and there, on the mountaintop, is my communications home for the next entire year.

We are approaching some kind of a small runway, I think. I hope. Through the tiny holes, where rivets used to be decades ago, I feel the chilling wind from the Arctic Ocean starting to get much stronger.

Just what is our miracle bush pilot doing by flying past a one-story building, right along the windows? I guess it is supposed to help keep the wind back. Everyone is waving to us from what looks like the inside of a dining room.

As we barely pass our shield against the wind, he is swerving our plane side to side, up and down. Or is it Mother Nature reminding us who's really flying this plane? Not us anymore. We are violently thrown sideways and headed for the Arctic Ocean. Our pilot struggles for enough control to swerve us back towards a very short beach. Another gust of wind tilts one wing toward the frozen sand. Our only remaining engine struggles to right us, but I can see we are not going to land gracefully on our wheels.

A wing tip, an engine, and a wheel all bite into the solid sand at once. With a sudden, back-breaking jerk, we are upside down with the frigid Arctic waters lapping at our heads. All the crates are tearing away from the cabin walls. My luggage and my freed chicken friends are violently propelled towards me now. All I can do is raise my shaking hands across my face and pray. Then, with a sledgehammer of pain crashing into my brain, Black Arctic night descends upon my conscious mind and my world of reality disappears.

Mentor Melvin

During David's days of recovery from his airplane crash and the resulting concussion, WAR once again seizes the chance to haunt David.

"I know you hate to fly, especially when your plane crashes, and does that exciting flip-over landing on the beach. I thought that would almost scare you to death. One of my better plans, if I do say so myself!"

David struggles to speak, but as yet cannot. His mind struggles for some thought and explanation. *What's happened and where am I?*

WAR starts to frighten him again, but then Melvin, David's subconscious Protector and Conscience, at last arrives for their first meeting. "Michael has sent me to help you in your battles against all your dark demons, including this treacherous WAR," Melvin informs David.

Melvin, as David's Protector and Conscience, can

assume the spiritual or physical form of anybody or anything, or both at the same time. To David, Melvin appears to only be a second-class wizard sent to aid him. WAR sees him as weak and not much of a threat to his battles for David's soul. But, it is only a mask to keep David from knowing his real mission, and so keep the truth from WAR. Melvin can disclose to David many secrets of the North to help in his battles with WAR.

For now, though, Melvin's presence is enough to send WAR scurrying away. He must retreat and reconsider his strategy. He wants to watch Melvin and devise the best plan of attack against David now that he is not alone. Without WAR to torment and try to kill him, David is able to start regaining consciousness.

Boy, do I have a headache. I remember something about a very bumpy landing. I'm a little groggy right now. Maybe that explains the very strange dream that hit me last night. It seemed so real, including all those visions of strange spirits, creatures, and even flying chickens, in my head. I know I'm in some kind of strange bedroom but how did I get here? Since I was so tired after flying all those thousands of miles, I wonder if I finally fell asleep on the plane and some kind person carried me to my room? Not likely, but there are all my suitcases. Smelly chicken clothes or not, I have to get some sleep. I'll change tomorrow. Very confusing.

My Tar Paper Shade

My mind is wandering so badly maybe I should try to finally concentrate on something, like my crazy-looking room. It's not much to look at. It's certainly not the Hilton. *Like it or not, here I am.*

Over my one and only window I see a weather-beaten, tar paper-like shade. It looks like those used during World War Two at night to keep the light in a room from being seen outside. In England, especially, this stopped the German bomber airplanes from using the glowing lights as a way to find their targets. *But why use them here?* I wonder. *Are we expecting bombers from Russia? I hope not, at least not during my first night, or maybe first day, here.*

It now dawns on me the dark shade is not used to keep the light inside from going outside, but just the reverse. It keeps the light outside from getting in. I have to remember that this is the land of the midnight sun, so during the summer months—as short as they may be—the sun never sets. I can just see myself, after a hard day of battling wild animals, finally getting into my bed about midnight with the sun blasting through my window, glaring into my snow-blind eyes.

Since there is no department store that might have a new shade for me within 1,000 miles, and I'm not sure when I last had a really good night's sleep, I think I'll just forget about any little imperfections. I'll just pull it all the way down and hit the sack. Flopping down on my new bed, I can feel the stress, and even a little fear, starting to leave my aching body, but all the confusion is still with me.

I bundle up in my mothball-scented blanket and try to thaw out from my many days of Arctic sleigh rides just to get to this frigid Hell. I finally close my eyes for some well-deserved sleep. *I still don't know what's going on with me and this knot on my head. Why are there feathers all over my suitcases? Oh what I'd give for an aspirin right about now. I'll worry about those Russian Bombers making all that noise in my head tomorrow.*

My First Day

Wow, that night went past too fast. Just where am I? Oh, yes, in the Arctic. Yes, in the Arctic now. For a very, very long time. Only some kind of an idiot would leave his love behind for all this Arctic fun. Jerking awake, it's my first lucid day in Mother Nature's ice box. A quick shower, some clean and less smelly clothes, and then finally dressed with a smile plastered on my face. Someone is knocking on my door. It's time to go, but go where and how do I get there?

After days of an almost miraculous recovery that he does not remember, David finally meets Eddie. Each day this new friend has looked in on David, from the moment he first crashed on the beach.

Eddie is somewhat small, yet pleasant-looking, about the age David's brother would have been had he not been killed in War. Eddie introduces himself as David's driver to the radio site on top of the mountain.

An expert mechanic, Eddie explains his specialty is operating and maintaining the Arctic snow vehicles, especially the two he calls Weasels. Because of Eddie's apparently caring nature, David hopes that over their next year together he can have a friendship with Eddie like the one he had with George. With Eddie's help, he feels he just might be able to live and survive in the Arctic.

In a huge, strange-looking truck, we leave our base site, a place we have not even seen in full daylight yet. We struggle to climb a very narrow road blasted out of the side of a mountain that must be at least a million years old. This very first trip up is not a gentle tour on some yellow brick road. It looks very narrow for even just one truck to pass, and maybe you don't!

"Eddie, is there much excitement up here once we learn the routine?" Maybe some Alaskan animals should be around somewhere—but hopefully not too wild.

He answers, "Not much."

He must be a man of few words, but many actions, when needed. No sooner has my mouth come up with those fateful words "much excitement," when another question explodes.

"What is that thing coming to greet us around the corner?" It looks very angry.

Eddie tells me it is a buck Caribou. The Caribou is thumping on the dirt road, apparently trying to decide how much of a threat we are in this very large, crazy-looking truck. I think that if this very large, equally crazy-looking animal really tried, he could knock this truck—and both of us along with it—right off this mountain, where we are almost 4,000 feet up, give or take a few hundred feet. So who is counting right now? Not me!

He suddenly stops his pounding on the road. Thank goodness, it looks like he doesn't want to battle us after all, at least not today. I partially open my right side truck door, swing my camera over the top edge and snap a picture of my very first animal in the Arctic wild.

Suddenly, Eddie yells a lot of four letter words at me over the deafening noise of our truck. At the same time, he yanks me back into the truck, slamming and locking the door behind me. He then hollers something about it not being a south forty-eight state family petting zoo up here.

Starting to thank Eddie for his quick action, I am interrupted by the sight and sounds of our not-so-tame buck Caribou walking, then running as fast as a speeding bullet. Eddie hollers something about bracing ourselves for a full frontal impact. I guess some animals, especially wild ones, just don't like their pictures being taken. Here he comes, thundering straight at us, so very close that I think I can actually smell his breath and see myself reflected in his wild, angry, glassy eyes. Here comes the big hit, but instead, he abruptly swerves his half-ton body towards the side of the truck. *My* side!

I feel the massive rush of air coming at me, like being in front of a speeding train just before it flattens me into just another railroad tie. The air pressure coming from this giant beast painfully pushes against my eardrums, or is it the thunder of his hoofs pounding our only escape road into fine dust?

His horns dig into my door, with the chilling screech of nails on a chalkboard. Our giant of a truck begins to rock sideways and skid even closer to the edge of our very narrow road. I am waiting for the end of my life that has just begun, and I never even got my first paycheck yet. *Oh, that stupid picture.*

My New Arctic Office

The screeching from horns raking my metal door finally stops. Eddie and I quickly turn our heads backwards the best we can, without leaving the safety of our Sherman tank. Our not-so-friendly Caribou is finally past us and slowly trots to the side of the road. He gradually works his way down the mountain. I believe he is probably gloating about his victory over these invaders into his land. Now, he is out of sight at last. I hope he isn't having any second thoughts about coming back up to finish his attack.

"What Now?" I ask Eddie, trying to sound confident, though I am not sure what courage I have left.

"Well, David, you got to remember this has been their land for a very long time. We're the strangers in town up here. You have to be prepared to protect yourself from about anything big, and even bigger. That's why you carry that .44 Magnum on your hip. I hope you never have to use that pea shooter against the really big ones. You'll probably come up with the short end of the stick." Because this is the most he has spoken thus far, I am just beginning to detect the South Georgia drawl in Eddie's accent.

"Thanks for saving my life, Eddie, and thanks for the all that scary advice, I think."

"Think nothing of it, kid. Okay, it's only about a mile straight up, so let's try again to get to the top."

"What's this 'try,' Eddie?"

"Just joshing you, Dave, oops, David. You got to have something to laugh about up here when all the Caribou stuff hits the fan."

Eddie and I have the same idea, as I instinctively ram my right foot almost through the floor on my side. With the real throttle on his side, Eddie guns the engine and we are making our way up the mountain again, a lot faster than before. It almost smells as if he is burning rubber, but how can that be on this dusty dirt road? I really don't care to figure that out at this very moment in my life. I just pray I never see those piercing, angry Caribou eyes ever again. But, I guess I have to remember where I am, and this land is his home territory, not mine, for I'm just a visitor, even if it is for quite a while.

As we come around another bend, I feel I need a little laughter and start humming the old tune "We are coming around the mountain when we come."

I wonder just how many "coming arounds" we have left on this groove called a road. How many miles of twists and turns have we come through so far, and how many more Caribou battles will we have until we finally reach my "new job"? No sooner do I utter that classic phrase to myself, *Are we there yet,* when we come around another curve and we are finally here. Well, almost.

I can see a silhouette against the early morning sky some distance ahead, made of strange-looking buildings and antennas. I'm supposed to know something about these giants and to be able to fix them if they break. *Just who do the big bosses think I am? Einstein?*

How desolate the perfectly flat landscape ahead looks compared to the constant mountain we have been traveling. Traversing those last few twists and turns just before finally reaching our buildings looks dangerous enough to maneuver on a semi-sunny day like today. I can just imagine how treacherous these same curves will be to handle in the dead of winter, soon to come, with all the wind and snow blowing across that flat mountain top. No mountain shelter here.

After turning the corner and driving through the last mountain pass, still covered with a dusting of early winter snow, we are finally here. Eddie skids to a full stop, jumps out of the truck, and makes a mad dash for the closest building and the first door he can find, betting on the safety of a very strong building to stop our charging Caribou friend. I was going to ask him about how I got from the airplane to my room last night, but I guess this is no time for me to interrupt him. I'll ask him later. Instead, still in some shock myself, I am really more intrigued with my new Arctic world than I am concerned with my safety at this very moment. I hope I don't later regret what I'm doing.

I get out of the truck to take a better look at this monster of a vehicle that must have come from another planet. It looks a lot different than it did in the dawn's early light thousands of feet below. Just what is all that extra equipment installed on it used for, anyway? I guess I will find out sooner or later, after some terrible Arctic Hurricane, when I am plowing through 50-foot snow drifts, steering clear of possible avalanches, all alone.

I soon see my new workplace up close. It has a very large radar dome and an equally large number of strange-looking radio antennas, some may even be seven stories tall. I am warned that if I stand too close these super-power microwave systems can damage, or even *fry,* a lot of my body parts. Then, looking around me, I find myself perched on top of a desolate, barren mountain overlooking the majestic and strangely beautiful Arctic Ocean. In this early rising sun, I can see the lonely little village I now call my home.

I must remember that even though it's only August here, the seasons are stranger than fiction—June, July and Winter. Just a trace of white, clean snow slowly forms on the peaks of our one and only mountain, the only one for 500 miles. It is both a land of beauty and one of fear of the unknown—a strange world that I have yet to discover.

Not long from now, the Arctic Ocean will slowly form its miniature icebergs, shimmering like giant diamonds. When they finally do, it is their destiny to be joined together to create a full ocean of solid ice. This journey begins as the early winter sun sinks lower and lower in the frosty Alaskan sky. As awe-inspiring as it may be to a *chechako*, a newcomer, like me, I already suspect that this northernmost ocean is certainly not a place for an early morning dip at *any* time of the year.

What a day my first one has been at my new home in the Arctic. At this rate, I can only imagine what my second day will be like. Probably fun and games with some smelly Polar Bear or slimy Walrus, or maybe even finding some lost Penguins.

I'm still in shock over what has really happened to me this very first day of the many hundreds left in my new Arctic home. I struggle to remember if my first day on the job is real or imagined. Stress and fear of tomorrow brings on another of my dreaded post-traumatic visions of George's violent death. How many more near-death experiences like this must I survive before I get back to my real home, if I even make it back?

New Friend's First Walk

Over my shoulder I see Eddie coming towards me from the main building. I know he is more shook up than I am, for he is the one who battled that beast with his truck, trying to keep it on the road. I know he's now somewhat relieved in more ways than one.

"I talked to the supervisor," Eddie says, "and told him the story about what we got into with that dumb Caribou your first day. He said you haven't even had a chance to see what's going on around here yet. You'll meet your partner, Lee, on the hill tomorrow. Let's take a tour, since we got light for a long time still. A walk will help us get to know each other, Dave."

As nice as Eddie is I feel he knows more about the threats looming around every corner of this God-forsaken place than he wants to tell me just now. I will find out more about who Eddie is and where he comes from as we walk and talk. So, we hop back into that monstrous truck with all the junk on it. I'll find out what it's for someday. Oh well, it's just an everyday truck with a big boom hoist, no springs, and no muffler. I hope the neighbors don't mind all the noise.

Off the narrow dirt road and finally at the bottom of the mountain, Eddie shows me this big pool of water.

"What's that for, Eddie?"

"That's our freshwater that comes from the melting snow as it trickles down underneath the permafrost. It also comes from little streams under the snow that form large creeks that gouge out the road, making it very narrow and very dangerous to drive on. All the water runs into this holding pond. We put stuff in it to keep the germs out, but that's it. What you see is what you drink. The construction guys did the best job they could burying the pipes to the base site in a really deep, heated trench. The pond doesn't freeze, except on the top."

Eddie then points at the buildings that will be our home away from home for a long time to come.

"Hey, Dave, did you notice the little trap doors across the roofs on the buildings when you flew over them coming in? Well, just pray that we don't have the kind of snow I guess they get around here once in a while. It gets so deep that it buries the dumb building and the crew has to come and dig us out. After a really big snowfall, they go up, open the trap doors, get the dozers and the shovels, and make paths to the real doors. As you saw from the air, except for getting up the mountain, we don't really have to do that much outside because the buildings are stuck together. You just go down one corridor and another corridor. It's really amazing, a real maze. That's supposed to be funny. A new fella like you could probably get lost for days. Just joshing you, Dave. Don't worry, I'll find you."

After Eddie finishes telling me about the submarine-type escape doors on the roof, we walk a little further, and he tells me to look up.

"See those strange signs, Dave, with arrows pointing in different directions? They have different words and things. Just a touch of home for us lonely fellas. They're like road signs. They're pretty much all pointing in about the same direction, towards the South 48, now 49, states where most of us call our real home. You don't see much of any pointing up north, except the one that says 'North Pole.'"

As I look closer at the signs, I tell Eddie, "I don't see anything that says 'Chicago.'"

"Nope, I think you're the first one, so if you talk to Bob—the key fixer upper around here—he'll probably put one up for you."

"Thanks, Eddie. It's a nice thought, but I have too many other things messing up my mind today, like giant Caribou."

As we turn around Eddie asks, "You see the buildings over there, that one separated from the rest? In the

Army it's called the motor pool, but that's our one-building workshop. That's where Bob hangs out trying to keep all this old World War Two-reject equipment running. He tries his best to keep the trucks and the Weasel track vehicles running. I bet you had those in your training in Anchorage."

"Yes, I did, Eddie. We learned how to drive them there."

"Well, Dave, those are my pets. Yep, the Weasels are pretty much my territory, and the bosses look to me to keep them running and maybe save our lives from the cold and them Polar Bears, even the Abominable Snowman. Just kidding about that Snowman, Dave. Okay, they got a heater in there that works most of the time, maybe too much sometimes. It gets a little hard to get some parts these days. You just don't have any auto store any place closer than about 1,000 miles. But, we make do with what we got or can make from scratch.

Otherwise, it's all got to be flown in or come by ocean barge. It can't be trucked in 'cause there ain't no roads, just the one that goes back up to the mountain. Well, we can always walk. Let's take a short one along the beach. You notice that I call you 'Dave?'"

"I did notice that Eddie. My name is really David. What's your real name?"

"Edward, but I hate it, 'cause it's too fancy for me, being from simple farming country in South Georgia."

"I did some army training in Georgia."

"Well, what a coincidence, Dave. Tell you what, everybody up here can call you David, but to keep your name from being fancy, I'll just call you Dave. Okay?"

"You got it, Edward, oops, just kidding, Eddie."

"When we walk a little further down the beach you're going to notice these telephone poles stuck in the ground, kind of like the ones around our buildings. But as we go further, you'll see a really strange, cockeyed thing about them poles. They kind of lean. Then, you go a little further and there ain't no wires on them because they busted off with the ice. Then there's just a big pile of rotten ones laying around with some others floating out to the ocean when the tide is right.

"You see, some bright young guy came up here from the south a long time ago and said he was going to run telephone poles from here all the way up to Point Barrow. That's a few hundred miles to the east. Everybody that knew anything about the far north kept telling him it just wasn't going to work. Maybe you can tell me why."

"Let me think about it for a minute, Eddie." I think Eddie is just testing my knowledge of this Arctic place. "It's the permafrost."

"Smart boy, Dave. We're going to get along fine, because you got some common horse sense. He put the dumb poles in the ground and within about a year they would just pop right back up again, and maybe even move 100 feet one way or the other. Even if they stayed in the ground and moved just a little, all those solid wires would just pop right apart. No wires. No phone calls. Yep, some darned fool tried it and it all went 'pop.' Just a dumb joke, Dave. Just shows you how dumb you can be when you don't understand how to live with Mother Nature up here in God's country."

We stop walking.

"That's about as far as we can go and not fall into the freezing Arctic. Oh yeah, you can always walk on the ocean water to the North Pole, but it better be a mighty cold winter and the water frozen solid. It's not like the South Pole that you can walk on any time because it has land underneath all that snow."

"Hey, Eddie, was that my refresher course about permafrost?"

"Yep. It ain't back home, you know, so you better stay on your toes around here. Not really, because they'd freeze in a wink at 50 below."

Eddie then says, "Now, remember which side of you the water's on, because that's the only way you'll know where you're going."

"Well Eddie, don't we know which direction we're going when we get turned around?"

"Now, Dave, you think about it. You're supposed to be a smart guy, and I been told that you were number one in your class there in Anchorage. You tell me what's going on with compasses up here."

"A compass is Caribou huntng standard equipment when you're walking around and you don't want to get lost."

"Okay, Dave, tell me about what you first thought of our Arctic world, then what you learned about your compass up here."

"Hey, is this a test to make sure I don't get lost when I'm out, roaming around this beach on my own, alone? Okay, if it makes you happy, teach," I shrug.

"Let's start with Arctic Wilderness Lesson 101. I use this word 'wilderness' loosely since, to me, it conjures up visions of glorious vegetation and gigantic trees. That's difficult to remember, when reality tells me the nearest tree, or even a bush, is over 500 miles beyond the most southern horizon. It is also difficult to realize that the magnetic North Pole is not actually 'up' from here."

"I can only wonder, if somehow stranded where I now stand, could the great world travelers of the distant past comprehend the mystery of how or even why their life-saving invention would point, not north, but 'sideways,' and even a little 'down south.'"

"Yes, it is a strange land where not only man, but his trusted compass thinks the world has turned upside down. As the great explorers of the past discovered the compass, the miracle of their time, just maybe, sometime, somewhere, someone, will discover a far more magical and dependable system. It would be a very accurate system that will tell travelers where they are anywhere on the entire earth, without depending upon the confusing Magnetic Pole."

"When I was a kid, I remember the joy of discovering new ideas and ways of overcoming difficult problems. Creating radios from oatmeal boxes. Mechanical moving ships and mountains, and electric toy cars, all gave me the thrill of maybe becoming a real inventor someday," I say, daydreaming.

Food Barge Arrival

"You know what, Eddie? Someday there might be some things I can help build that will be better for world travelers than a compass."

Eddie assures me, "Oh, I know you will, kid." *Well, how does he know my future?*

"When did you get up here, Eddie?"

"I just got here the day before you."

If only the day before me, how does he know so much about this place? How does he know about the crazy animals up here, like that Caribou we met? I ask him, "Did you know everything about this place before you got up here? You know so many things!"

"Well, Dave, I read a lot." *I wonder what he reads.*

"Maybe you can't tell a lot about people, like me, just from the way they look and the way they talk."

Eddie doesn't answer.

Continuing our walk and getting further away from

the base camp, I wonder about what time we need to get back in order to return before dark.

As if reading my mind, Eddie tells me, "We still got a lot of light but, you know, you have to watch it because it's still getting later and we don't want to miss the boat."

"The boat? What boat?"

He reminds me, "We started walking with the Arctic Ocean on our left, so let's turn around and now keep the Arctic Ocean on the right. Because if the ocean's still on our left, we would wind up walking hundreds of the miles to Point Barrow. You remember the story about Point Barrow don't you? Who were the couple of flyers?"

"Yeah, I remember a little from school books. There was Will Rogers, who was a great comedian during the 1930s and 40s. He had a pilot friend, named Wiley Post, who had only one good eye."

"Yeah, they came up here to take a tour and do some

hunting, but crashed just outside Point Barrow and both died. Many believe their spirits still haunt the place, so watch yourself if you ever fly to Point Barrow, 'cause you may not quite make it back. We have good bush pilots up here, but Rogers and Post just weren't used to flying in this strange Arctic weather. Anyway, let it be a warning to you if you go flying around here. You can get into trouble. So, let's keep the Arctic Ocean on the right and you look out there. You don't see much ice or anything yet do you?"

"No."

"Well, just wait around a little bit, when it gets to be winter out there. In Anchorage they told you there are just about three seasons—June, July, and Winter—up here, and that's pretty much right. You can walk around in a T-shirt when the sun's up in the middle of July, but don't try that in the middle of September. You get your woollies and stuff on because it's going to freeze your butt off by then. Some years there are some strange storms and some strange snow, and you can't see more than about a mile at best. The wind comes in with the moisture and the water from the Arctic Ocean and crawls up the mountain. Next thing you know, it's snowing or foggy on the mountain, but not down here. Then, it can be foggy down here and no fog up there. That means you really got to watch yourself when you travel on that road, trying to see and not drive off the side of the mountain."

"That's good advice, Eddie"

"Glad you got that, Dave. It might save your life up here someday. Let's keep walking and go around this last turn to a little hill crop out. Look hard to see something special."

"Lo and behold, off in the distance, I see something in the Arctic Ocean and two dots."

"Yep. It will be a little while before we can really see

what's out there. We'll just slow down a little and talk about what's going to happen over the next year to both of us. Why do we work up here? Why are you here, Dave? Don't tell me. I'll figure it out later."

We continue walking back to the base camp.

Eddie says, "Well, you'll find out that we have a number of fellas working different shifts because we have to keep the communications and radar place running twenty-four hours a day, seven days a week, or the bad boys will attack us. Since we're the closest ones to them, they will get us first. There is a saying up here 'The first to know and the first to go' if a War ever starts. That's us, Dave.

"They're going to target us, knock us out and take over from here, then go on down the Alaskan coast, taking the rest of our Arctic brothers out. That's why we're pretty important up here, to stop 'em. Don't go thinking you're just another one of the regular people up here. Oh, no. We're up here for a reason, and it may be that we have to really do the thing we got to do. That is, we may be the ones getting our comeuppance up here, if it turns out that we really get into a War. Yeah, that's why we have three work shifts, because we have to make sure that somebody's fresh on duty.

"It can be a little tiring up here, especially when it gets really dark and cold outside, even in the building. There's always two, and maybe even three, up there at one time. I don't think you ever want to be caught up there by yourself. Sometimes it takes a couple of people to fix all that technical stuff, and you're one of them. When you're up there, don't worry, though, because Lee's up there a lot. He's the manager."

"Thanks for all the happy news, Eddie."

"You're welcome, Dave."

"Okay, Dave, enough of that fun stuff. Take a look way out there again and look at what we see. Them little dots have become three ships. They will be coming up on the beach soon. The little boat is called a tug, pulling the big one, called a barge. They can come up with supplies only once a year before the Arctic Ocean freezes over and locks us in for about a year. Then, they come back again next summer when everything thaws out. Just think about all the goodies we're going to have over the next many months when they get done unloading it. They will put it in the big food locker here. Well, not really.

"We have generators for electricity, and those generators keep the big heater in the big antennas going to keep your old fanny warm in that big building up there. It's the same for the guys in the radar dome and down here, but you can't waste electricity on cooling machines. You see, were sitting on the side of a mountain that's made of ice at least a million years old. When this place was built, they blasted a hole in the side of the mountain right behind all the buildings. That became our frozen food locker. We just simply built the storage building right into that. That's where Cookie makes his great meals. You'll meet him later. He keeps all of the food and everything that can spoil in his big Mother Nature freezer."

"So, Eddie, we don't really have or need a real electrical freezer?"

"You got it. It's a real Ice Box. That's a joke for us farming folks that still take a dump outside in a smelly little house and use blocks of ice to keep things cold. Yep, just part of the mountain that stays cold all the time with nothing else needed."

"So, Eddie, we really just need a smart Cookie making our food. What's his name?"

"As I said, Dave, you will meet him later. He's got a real name, but nobody knows what it is. Maybe it's even top secret. Maybe it's Elvis or something. Let's walk ahead the rest of the way and we can watch a little bit more of the barge bringing the food in. I can just taste some of that great stuff for the next number of months because it's all safe and sound and ready to eat. You know, it won't be too long until it's Thanksgiving and Christmas and we will have some of that great beef and other food they bring to us on the barge."

David thanks Eddie for the tour and the trip. He still wonders how his new friend knows all these things if only arriving a day before him, but David has a good feeling about Eddie. Maybe even that friendship he desires is forming.

"Yep, I'm looking forward to all that good food coming in off that barge before they head on back down south.

We're the last site on their last run before those fellas get to go home for their Thanksgiving and Christmas. Sure, there's airplanes to come in, and they bring stuff in, but not eggs in the dead of winter because they freeze. So they bring in the chickens. You get the eggs for a while, and when they get old you get to eat old chicken. So, yeah, you get some fresh stuff now and then if you got a good bush pilot."

"Eddie, what does 'fresh' mean?"

"Don't know, but the main stuff comes in on the barge just once a year. Don't worry, Dave, it will be safe in Cookie's ice mountain food locker. After all, it's been there a million years without melting, probably will be a million more."

I have a strange feeling about all this vital food just stuck in the side of a frozen mountain, surviving an entire year and think, *Maybe not. Eddie, Maybe not.*

The next morning, Eddie and I get to the mountain

site. This time, without any Caribou battles. There, I finally meet Lee and begin my training on the actual communication equipment on top of this mile-high mountain I'd soon learn to call "The Top." I am supposed to be an expert in keeping all this fancy electronics stuff alive. *Sure.* All that book learning and lab work back at the Anchorage training school for three months is one thing, but now I have been thrown into the "fix it or maybe die" national defense world.

All my life, since my father deserted me, I've had to make my own way. By now I'm tired of doing everything myself, alone, especially in this world of unbelievable isolation. I'm sure glad I have Lee to help me out, and all the other really smart technicians who have been here much longer than I have. I hate being alone.

Birthday Home Sick

I have just a month of added equipment training that keeps me very busy, and I learn our mission on the Cape well. But now it's September, which means the beginning of real Arctic snow. It's my birthday, September 4, 1959, to be exact.

At the age of 24, I am not too old to be homesick. I take a walk on the beach, look up at my "home" on top of the mountain, and have visions of the last time I saw my family and my love, Annie. My PTSD is getting worse with the increasingly dark days, but I force myself to reject even thinking about quitting and going back home. If I go back, I will lose the dream funds I came up here to earn. It would be so easy to just leave everything behind and get on the next plane for home.

I know somewhere, far beyond the Northern Lights and the Midnight Sun, and almost hidden from sight, is a marvelous Arctic world yet to be discovered. Soon, though, I will no longer be able to see any of this beauty and magic, for the sun I know and remember will begin its long, deep Arctic winter sleep. Many cold, desolate months will pass before our sun will be reborn and fully light the sky and warm the plants and animals of the Earth.

It has not been that long since I first arrived in this foreboding world of cold. Yet, I already begin to feel the same loneliness and need for the touch and comfort of my own human mate, just as I believe any Arctic beast would feel for his in this desolate land of the far North.

I especially dream of the tender touch of the one I love and left far behind in that airport an eternity ago. I know my many battles to survive in this God-forsaken place have just begun. How many more such challenges like that plane crash and that dance with the Caribou will there be for me before this same time next year, when I will have consumed almost a third of my life here on earth?

I know I must learn to adapt to my new life where I now live, and may even die. But, for now, I cannot fill this empty hole in my heart and soul that longs for that small but loving space on Earth I call my True Home.

During his doubts about the terrible decision he made, just to be able to create a life together with Annie, David calls for someone to comfort him. There is no answer at first, but then Annie comes to him in his dreams that night. She reassures him of her complete faith in him and declares her unconditional love for him; she will wait forever for him to return to her. His mind at ease, he finally falls into a deep sleep.

Food Locker Destruction

It sounds like Eddie knocking on my Hilton room door; that's the inside joke up here. I know it's him by the funny way he does that rapping with his fingers, like he is milking a cow back on his farm.

"Come on in, Edward." He enters and just stares at me, but then smiles because he knows I only call him by his full name when I'm feeling pretty good and just want to tease him about calling me Dave.

"Hey, David, oops, Dave, let's go get some vittles. It's lunch time." Cookie has always been able to rustle up some mighty fine vittles, as Eddie would say.

Off we go to our not-so-fancy dining room, jokingly called a restaurant. As we approach, we hear some rumbling of voices from those who got there before us trying to beat the crowd.

Upon entering, some of the others see us and shout, "Hey, Evans, did you hear what happened to all that food we got off the barge last month, which is supposed to last us until the end of next year? Well, it ain't."

In the middle of all this confused chatter the base captain enters with a call to attention. He then breaks the bad news to us.

"Enough of all this scuttlebutt. I'm here to tell you the straight scoop. As you all know, there is no need to have an electric freezer to store our food up here, when we have a mountain made of million-year-old ice right behind us. For years that big hole blasted out of the ice right behind Cookie's cooking area has worked great to keep everything as fresh as we can. But, no longer. Just after our yearly food supplies got off the barge and were stored there, safe from all the bears, and ready for our delicious meals...no moaning, guys, about Cookie's fine cooking...there was a not-so-slight accident. One of the older bulldozers stored on the hill began to leak oil. It ran between the still-frozen permafrost layer and upper tundra soil, finding its way into our mountain-side food locker. The leak was so slow that nobody noticed it until now. A great deal of our food was ruined. Most of the good stuff off the barge didn't make it, and Cookie had to toss it. As you know the Arctic Ocean is starting to freeze over pretty much now. So, that's it for any more barge help.

"Yes, the better bush pilots can fly in some extra supplies, but it will be weight-limited and dangerous with all the Arctic winter winds starting up. The heavy stuff like meat is gone. No beef, ham, or turkey. It's going to be a pretty lousy Thanksgiving and Christmas without it. Now, as much as you hate messing with Mother Nature up here where we are only visitors, we need some kind of meat and protein or we'll all get pretty sick soon. I need some volunteers to hunt down some of our Caribou neighbors and lug them back here, after saying a prayer of thanks over their souls, as the

Eskimos believe you must do when taking a life.

"I must warn you, if you accidently run into an entire herd, this could turn into a very dangerous mission. Anybody stepping forward?"

I hear one courageous person jump up and say, "I WILL!"

Caribou Hunt

"Eddie, you're volunteering?"

"Yep, Dave."

Not to be outdone by my less-than-Einstein farmer friend, and knowing I may have to help run off a bunch of wild beasts as he did for me on that first day, I jump up and holler, "Me too!"

All of our less courageous friends stand up and applaud as our captain lets loose with a thank you and a great sigh of relief. We all know, with no volunteers, he would have the terrible duty of picking somebody, or wind up going himself.

Not knowing how far or how long into winter we would have to travel to accomplish our meat-hunting mission, Eddie and I round up all the Arctic clothing and survival gear we can carry. Maybe too much, when I realize somebody will have to lug back hundreds of pounds of literally dead meat.

"Eddie, just what do you know about chasing down wild animals and doing what you have to do to murder them?"

"Dave, you gotta remember I'm from farming country, with plenty of cattle and even some wild deer now and then. When times get tough, it's either them or you if you want to survive."

"That makes sense, Eddie, but who's going to do the hunting, killing, and taking out all the guts?"

"That's what I do, Dave."

"But, what do I do to help?"

"Well, somebody's got to lug back all this...what did you call it... dead meat? Guess who, city boy?"

"Okay, okay. I guess with only two of us I win by default."

"So, Dave, without all those fancy words, you know you got the short end of the stick."

"Eddie, you know what you had to do when you

rushed to our mountain building after we got attacked by that big Caribou on our first day? I feel just that way now, since I'm a little apprehensive, hell, really scared about what we're going to do now. Oh, God, I pray that first-day Caribou with the glassy eyes and smelly breath isn't still mad at me for taking his picture and waiting to ambush us just around the next corner."

"That's okay, Dave. If we do get attacked again and you wind up with brown stains on your underwear, we do have a washing machine back at the base."

"Oh, well, 'A man's got to do what a man's to do.' I think I heard that in an old John Wayne movie somewhere. Eddie, let's 'bite the bullet,' or bite the Caribou, and start hunting!"

"Okay, David, my little brother."

"Okay, Edward, my best friend. I sure hope they have lots of good soap for that washing machine."

Reluctant Christmas Preacher

One Sunday after church services, having become such good friends over many months, I joke with Father Deery about his conning me into doing his job once in a while. He calls my bluff and pulls me aside as if he has something important to say.

"What can I do for you, Father?"

"You know, David, I can't be everywhere up here in the Arctic to help everyone who has problems coping with all the isolation and loneliness this time of year. They want to be home with their families. With the winter weather getting worse, I don't want to put our bush pilot friends that fly me up here in any more danger than absolutely necessary. Your friends here think highly of you both for what you and Eddie did to bring home the meat, literally, on that much-needed Caribou hunt. They trust you because you so easily listen to them spill out their feelings, and they know you have come through a great deal in your few months with them. You have already given them simple Sunday worship when I can't be here. As I try to be part of the right hand of our God, I look to you to be my right hand in faith. I would like you to lead the prayer service at your Christmas celebration.

"I know you will do me and all your friends proud. I see in you something you may not know. You have a calling to help others through their pain and suffering. I see a marvelous future for you and your Annie in your world of love for each other and all those you meet. Will you do this Christmas prayer for me, and for God and all your searching friends, who are just trying to protect all they love from War as you have vowed to do?"

"Father, I feel so humbled by your asking. I would be proud to honor your request, and will remember your caring love all my life. Merry Christmas, Father Deery."

Alone for Eternity

February 1960 marks the midpoint of David's isolation in the Arctic. The first six months of the entire year of his commitment are behind him, but he will have to battle and survive the next six months before he can return to Annie with the critical funds they need for their life together. He has learned his job well at his small, but critical, classified military mountain post overlooking the Arctic Ocean. Hired as a long-range radio communications expert, he continues his mission of providing North American Defense Command with advanced knowledge of spies, saboteurs, and possible invasions across the North Pole from Russia.

I now have learned enough about all this complicated communications equipment to repair a few things, if needed, but there is so much more to know, so much to understand. I feel I can handle most uncertainties ahead of me if given enough time and added training. I am so thankful to have my fellow worker, friend, and mentor beside me. Leonard likes to be called Lee. He tells me Leonard is a rich man's name, but since he's a simple boy from a small town, to please use his simple name. Lee is a soft-spoken, mature, much "older" man, of at least 35. He is a great instructor, both thorough and very patient with me and my slow learning pace.

As we prepare a small lunch together, Lee tells me he is not feeling very well. Probably too much of that smelly Caribou meat. I find some stomach medicine in our emergency aid cabinet. He takes some of it, but says he's still in pain. I think we've had enough of this self-help doctoring, so I call down to the base camp and declare a medical emergency.

A medic tells me the weather report does not look good, with a winter storm coming, but he will send up their best driver. I know old, reliable Eddie is the one picked to rescue Lee. Since we always have two operating personnel on our site for every shift for safety and for emergency situations such as this, I know I will be with the very best fellow operator coming up with Eddie. One who will teach me new repair tricks like Lee always does.

I try to make Lee as comfortable as I can while waiting for Eddie and our relief person. Minutes seem like hours as Lee's condition worsens. Even with all the howling wind, I finally hear the noisy tracks of our snow vehicle, packing down mounds of rapidly falling snow. Everyone calls this rumbling miniature tank, left over from World War Two, a Weasel. I really don't care what it's called right now as long as it gets Lee back home to medical help.

I open the main door only a crack, and the wind violently rips it out of my hand, sucking much of the heat out of the building. Through the never-ending black of Arctic winter sky, I can imagine this strange Arctic storm is rapidly becoming a frigid Arctic tornado, forming directly over the radar dome.

Even in this driving snow, I can see Eddie hunched low, almost crawling face down, battling to reach me, but I don't see anyone else. Working together, with all our brute strength against the ever-growing wind, we finally are able to get Lee to the Weasel.

Struggling to open the passenger door, we carefully lift Lee inside and slam it shut. Eddie works his way to the other side, gets in, and slams his door against the driving wind. The rumbling engine still running from his trip up, Eddie turns the clanking machine around as I nervously wave goodbye to them both. I turn to see the last of our giant antenna disappear into a white world of nothingness and hope it will still exist tomorrow.

My eyes are almost covered with driving snow and sleet and nearly frozen shut. I battle to reach the small safety and warmth of our quaking station. With all of my remaining strength, I manage to slam the wide open door shut against the blustering wind.

Our courageous Eddie came up for Lee, but brought nobody else to take his place. I can only imagine the challenges against this storm they must have down at the base just to keep our home in one piece. They probably need every able-bodied man, too. Maybe they all think I am pretty good at running this place, which is okay by me most of the time. But, with an Arctic winter storm from Hell like this coming, I'm not so sure I can keep this vital electronic communication station up and running alone.

David has relied on Lee and other friends during his months of continued training, and when relief doesn't come to fill in for Lee, the menacing storm becomes even more frightening.

However, he knows he must keep the radio system working no matter what. He performs his list of duties, checking everything over. He then sits down at the lunchroom table and wonders why he has not received any mail in the last two weeks, even though two planes had arrived, bringing mail up to Lee. Has Annie's unconditional love for him dissolved with her waiting so long for him to return to her, so much longer than when he was away in the army?

Even though they are now thousands of miles apart, he feels her sad thoughts. He remembers that, even after her impulsive journey to see him in New Jersey and the many letters she wrote him, he never wrote back.

Annie's Memories, Letters and Disaster

"Oh, such happy, then sad, memories, Wayne. As luck would have it, your sister, Dolores, and family were taking your car to you at your army post in New Jersey and they invited me to go along. Of course, I jumped at the chance and told my parents I was going all the way to New York City. New Jersey or New York was all the same to me, as long as I could be with you, my Soldier Boy, again.

So, here this young girl, me, took off with these people I hardly knew. My parents were quite supportive of me, never questioning my trip. Once in New Jersey, we all went to New York City for one night and I saw my first Broadway play.

All too soon our second real date ended and I was leaving you again, this time on a train back to Indiana. With no more leaves or visits for a long time to come, we had to be satisfied with writing letters.

At first I wrote you every day but didn't mail my letters, waiting for you to write me. Well, you didn't, and I was crushed.

David is saddened at the memory of how he treated Annie then, even though he did finally write her again. Having to push the memory aside, though, David realizes it has been many hours of waiting and that the weather is getting even worse. He checks the doors and windows. All secure, but weakening. Since the power cables are buried deep in the mountainside, he will have life-giving warmth and light as long as the generators far below at base camp stay alive.

So it is, too, with the buried telephone and teletype

cables from the radar dome 1,000 yards away, between his own communication building and the base camp. There is only one place where these critical wires rise out of the ground to be connected together—in a small, isolated closet, out of sight and out of mind.

With the equipment shaking, even greater wind speeds, and lower temperatures, David begins to put on the first of many layers of Arctic clothing. Not much later, still waiting for added help to come for his relief, he begins to realize that even with Eddie's expertise of traveling in ice, snow, and wind, relief from below is beyond reality.

With Hurricane Winds and extreme cold, the radio communication systems begin to fail. Conditions getting worse, he finally understands his disintegrating communication site is for him to keep alive... alone."

The Russians Are Listening

In the meantime, in the Bering Strait, off Alaska's coast, on a strange-looking fishing trawler, two young Russians are spying on David's communication site by monitoring his ever-weakening radio signals to Kotzebue.

"Alexis, Alexis!!! Their radio signal is almost gone. What does it mean? Why is it happening?"

"Practice English, Boris! English. Hold on, now. We have to be absolutely certain this is a serious matter. We cannot report this to Moscow and have it turn out to be a false alarm. A lot of terrible things could happen to us if we are wrong. You know it could just be the weather or that our antennas are not in the right position. But do you know what it means if their signal is really down? We must check everything and be absolutely sure. If it's just strange signal interference, from our stand point, this does not mean we should blow it up to more than it is. Keep checking the signal and see if we can pick it up again. We better check everything twice. Hurry, now!"

Soon, the constant chatter between the radar dome operators (just 100 yards away) and the support team at the base camp far below is gone. All calls of danger from the mile-high mountaintop to the outside world become nothing but deafening silence.

David then realizes he is not really alone. Doctor Varian, his inventor friend from the Anchorage training center comes to his mind, repeating the doctor's warning about his Klystron transmitter tubes' temperature problem. "If they get too hot, they will burn up. If they get too cold, they will stop working altogether. That's why there is a special cooling system for them."

David realizes that with the room's temperature already at freezing, the cooling fluid still pumping around the critical transmitter tubes may soon freeze and cause the tubes to die. But, if he turns off the pump, thus stopping the cooling fluid, the tubes may stay just warm enough to transmit some small level of radio signals. That way, somebody further south will realize he is still alive and that the transmitter building has not been blown off the mountain into the Arctic Ocean—yet.

With no way to call for help, and nobody to ask for guidance, he must, once again, make the terrible decision...alone. He must disobey all government rules he has vowed to honor. If it works in keeping some radio signal alive and he survives, he may be honored as a hero. If it fails and the tubes are destroyed, his reckless action may brand him a saboteur and traitor.

Gritting his chattering teeth, he turns the pump off.

NORAD Screams

Meanwhile, deep inside an isolated desert mountain in Colorado, it is near chaos at the United States North American Defense Command Center known as NORAD. Here, the National Emergency Alert goes off with deafening screams.

"Captain, get that damn noise turned off! It's probably just another of the thousands of tests we have had to live through since this stupid cave was first built years ago. While you're at it, find out what the hell is going on. Just to be safe, seal the center. Nobody enters. Nobody leaves."

"Yes, General."

"Well?"

"It's a real alert, General."

"Where?"

"Alaska, sir."

"Well, Captain, that's a mighty big place. Can you be just a little more specific?"

"It's our White Alice Coastal Radar warning system protecting the upper west coast, facing Siberia."

"How bad?"

"We have lost all communication above the Kotzebue Air Force Base radar site."

"So, you're telling me, Captain, for the first time ever, our early warning communication system facing those damn Russians has a busted link?"

"Yes, General."

"Where is it?"

"The Cape."

"Isn't that the uppermost site, right on the Arctic Ocean?"

"Yes, General."

"Do we know why it has crashed?"

"Our weather people guess it's probably due to a major Arctic storm."

"How bad?"

"The last known communications from there reported one-hundred-twenty-five-mile-an-hour winds with a real temperature of eighty below zero."

"Those poor souls. They may all be blown off the mountain and frozen to death by now. How long have they been down?"

"Almost a day, General."

"So, Captain, with our super intelligence system, we are just now hearing about it? With the damn Russians just a stone's throw across the Bering Sea from the Cape, their spies probably know more about what's going on up there than we do!"

"Maybe, General."

"There is no maybe about it. We don't know what kind of a spy operation they have up there, but maybe this mess-up will be just the thing to cause them to slip up and we can flush them out."

"General, that would be a major breakthrough for our intelligence team."

"Yeah, and we may only wind up sacrificing over a hundred of our best people up there to get this information. A pretty lousy trade off, Captain."

"How long has our system been down, and us blind to their intentions? How long would it take for the Russians to take some serious action against us?"

"I'd give them three days before that tickle up their butt about our site failure turns into a full-blown gas pain and they would explode in our direction."

"Do you mean a preventive strike?"

"That's called invasion, son. Finally, the 'Big One' that nobody in their right mind would ever want to start."

"Where would they come from, sir?"

"Over the top, Captain, and Santa couldn't stop them. What's the weather report at the North Pole?"

"Our best information, without the Cape's radar, is just about clear."

"Oh, even if our guys are still alive, they are socked in

by that damn storm and couldn't even see what hit them. I know this super-secret communication equipment isn't worth a damn right now, but can't we call them on a plain, old stupid telephone?"

"No, sir. Phone poles and wires can't be installed in the Arctic ice. That's why we put in that long-range radio system."

"Once again, 'for the lack of a nail'...never mind. You're too young to know what I am talking about. Well, we don't have much of a choice but to pray those fellows up there are still alive and are smart enough to repair the damage when the storm is finally over. I even hope the Russians really are spying on us some way and know when we are back up and our radar is watching every move they make again. It's frightening to even think how less than three days could make or break us, and maybe even the whole damn world."

"General, they were all handpicked to go up to this

site because of their superior technical knowledge and ability to work under pressure."

"Well, Captain, if they don't get their butts in gear pretty soon, they will really know what pressure is, especially when fighting off the Russians. Who is the most experienced person up there who can take over and make things happen fast? Look him up."

"The top student in the latest Anchorage training class, with a great deal of additional communications knowledge is named Evans."

"I sure hope he is as good as he thinks he is, with the guts to stay alive and lead the others to find the mental and physical limits they need to create a miracle, for all of us."

Russian Decision and Radiation

"Hey, Boris, maybe we could just wait a little while to report to Moscow this dying radio signal, and now no more voice warning messages from their radar to their officers at their North American Defense Command headquarters. Instead, let's just tell all this to our air force and make it their responsibility."

"Yes, Alex, the planes can get much closer and see what has really happened to the Cape site during the storm. If the radio signal and voices come back soon, let the air force tell Moscow that it was all the fault of the stormy weather and take the blame for such a false alarm. This could be the beginning of a real War and we don't want to be responsible for being the messengers that started it all and suffer the consequences."

With no calls from his Arctic home below, David imagines giant Arctic Ocean winds have torn their giant white radar balloon into ancient ship sails, stripped from a towering mast. Now, wrapped in their personal white burial sheets, born from the cloth that remains of the dome, he believes all his friends have been hurled off the mountaintop into the deep catacombs of the ocean floor.

In David's disintegrating mountain refuge, the last life blood of human warmth is being sucked out of him as the wind whistles through every widening crack and crevice, creating the screams of 1,000 bats. Even shreds of his undershirt jammed deep into his ears cannot keep the growing deafness away. The shattered glass of small observation windows becomes arrow-sharp shrapnel hurled into his thick but fragile parka. The comforting glow of the electric lights, once powered by giant buried cables and massive generators, flicker in a dance with death.

After what feels like an eternity of freezing and struggling to keep some semblance of life in his failing communication system and himself, David collapses on a table. He is forced to be next to the only source of warmth he has left, the lethal-powered radio transmitter. Its protective doors have been torn open by the violent shaking of the building.

The dying, but still powerful, giant transmitter tubes spew forth deadly radiation. The same lethal forces of human annihilation unknowingly leashed upon mankind by the first Atomic Bombs used to end World War Two.

Should he miraculously survive his battle with Nature, this radiation is destined to destroy his seed of life and so condemn his children never to be born.

In his growing delusions, he believes that all those he loves are condemned to die by his failure. As his freezing lips quiver a last goodbye, he knows death is his fate, and asks all he may have sinned against to forgive him.

Freezing Death

With David on the verge of giving up, WAR's work will be easy. David has almost done the job himself, so WAR does not have to push him much further to get him over the edge, to get him to give up and die.

Playing on David's constant fear of dying at War, WAR tells David to finally surrender, "Freezing to death, David, can be a peaceful ending to all your battles with me. This truly is your destiny. Accept your life of failures and that the Russians will soon discover your site's radar warning systems no longer exist, and your vision of an invasion by them will come true."

David knows it is now his turn to enter the depths of Hell. He believes this will be the final meeting with his personal Angel of Death, who he knows to be the evil spirit of all he hates, WAR.

Only six agonizing months are left before his return to Annie after their eternity of loneliness apart. It is a chilly, dark night in Annie's hometown of Whiting, Indiana. In a restless sleep, she struggles to comprehend her Soldier Boy David's life in the constant, freezing darkness of the Arctic.

Annie knows something is terribly wrong in David's world when a sudden chill of death overtakes her mortal soul. She tries desperately to shake away the nightmares of despair, but cannot. Even though thousands of miles apart, she has to get to him, as she feels his love for her disappearing. In her subconscious mind, she cries out to him to have the courage in this battle against the demon demanding his very soul in death.

Just as when she finally sent all her letters, after receiving none from him while in the army those many years ago, she takes control of her mind and shouts, "No, Not Now. Not in that terrible place. You must come back to me. You haven't even loved me yet."

As if a powerful electric shock hit his very soul, David

violently jerks back from his dark journey to eternal damnation.

"Yes, yes, my Annie. I feel your love for me alive again. I hear you. 'Not in this terrible place.'"

David forces his eyes open to see if the world still exists. He is alive again, and the screaming bats and violent shaking are deathly silent. Although badly damaged, the walls and roof of his communication building still exist. Even as dark and cold as he knows it still is outside, he feels a growing warmth in his body and soul.

"Thank you. Thank you, bright world. I am still alive to feel, to touch, to love. Thank you, my Annie, for believing in me and for your Unconditional Love."

Why *Not* Me?

It is only natural for humans to search for some true meaning to their earthly existence. The desire for fairness and fair play are part of mankind's moral fiber from birth.

As people go through life, many events occur that can cause them deep emotional struggles and much pain, either directly, or through friends and loved ones. When confronted with these difficulties and hard decisions, people automatically search inside themselves and base much of their actions on what is fair for them or for others.

When life takes a turn for the worse, dramatically affecting their well being, even to the point of the unexpected death of someone, the grief and anger felt by those left behind instantly results in cries of despair, "It's not fair!" They may feel that time and time again the world and all its people have turned against them. How many times must they shout, "Why?" "Why me?"

"Life is not fair!!!" Many times those suffering ask the question "Is life fair?" David too, now firmly believes that life is not fair, but for a totally different reason from those who have suffered so much and cried, "Why *me*?"

"Michael, when others may not have made it through each of my deadly ordeals, how and why did I? I firmly believe there must be a reason for me to still be alive. I must have a mission to accomplish while here on earth. What is it? I am still searching and surviving, and until I complete what I was sent here to do, I will never stop asking, 'Why *not* me?'"

"David, your journey of struggles here is not complete. You have much to learn on your path to find your inner self and your true reason for being, your destiny. Many secrets of life will be offered to you to accept or reject with your Free Will. Your journey will teach you a world of knowledge, but these are only the tools to use in discovering the true wisdom to better serve your world. Hate or forgiveness, loneliness or deep friendship, are some of the hard choices yet before you. Look to Melvin, whom I have sent to aid you as your friend and conscience. Heed his words wisely."

Melvin and Miracles

Still barely holding onto my small shaking table by the open transmitter doors, I hear a telephone ringing, or do I? Is this one of Melvin's tricks, as Michael said he would play, just to fool the dark side of my mind? I really can't hear sounds very well. My ears are still stuffed with pieces of my underwear. They were not much noise protection against all that screeching that came from every crack and crevice in this groaning, swaying building.

The more I become aware of my surroundings, the more I realize the building no longer feels as if it's being torn from its crumbling foundation. Almost three days and nights I was without sleep. Still in a daze, I feel this storm of the century must be subsiding, at least to some degree. The wind has dropped from 125 miles per hour at 95 below zero to a gentle 60 miles per hour, a mere breeze compared to its former self, though I don't think "breeze" is the right word yet.

I see the needles on our four receivers starting to rise just a tiny amount off zero. The dense, stormy sky must be thinning a little and letting our weak radio signal sneak through to the Kotzebue site over 300 miles away. I don't know yet if it is really a phone ringing or my wishful imagination. I take the pieces of my underwear out of my ears, probably very dirty and smelly after 3 days in this Arctic Hell.

I look down the main hall at a floodlight pointing my way. Some great scientist attached it to our phone line so it would flash when a call is coming in. As much as my groggy, frozen brain allows me, I strain to hear that friendly ring again, but I do not. My body groans with every move after days of freezing temperatures, and my blood is now as thick as Jell-O.

I must force myself to get off this table of death and do my best to close these radiation protection doors before my rescue arrives, if they are even still alive down at the base.

Melvin, keeper of my inner thoughts and strengths, where have you been when I needed you the most? What words of wisdom can you dig out of my still-confused mind?

"Wire."

"Why are?" Why are and then what? Oh, another one of your one-word games you like to play to try to make me smarter. You know I've had a pretty lousy past few days up here alone where my world was crashing around me. I could have used some help. So what have you to say for yourself?

"Wire!"

Not that "why are" thing again.

I finally understand. *Melvin, old friend, it's not "why are;" it's "wire." OK, so what am I supposed to do with this piece in information? I know, I'm supposed to save the world now. Sure.*

Now mentally and physically strong enough to fully rouse myself, I know what Melvin is saying. Even better, I am finally able to move and speak.

"Okay, Melvin, I'm up. It's time for you to tell me what's really going on between us, even though I've finally figured it out myself. But how can anything be wrong with the wires? They are all buried in this mountain, except for where they come out of the ground into the wire closet. Wire closet?

"Once all the phone and Teletype wires were attached, there was no reason for me or anyone else to go back in there. I don't even remember where that closet is. After all, there is nothing in there but stupid telephone wires. Telephone wires? Stupid? Melvin, anytime I doubt your one-word wisdom, you have the right to call me a big, fat dummy. I'll just pretend I didn't hear that 'yes' coming from you, Melvin. Just remember, Michael tells me you live in my mind. That means you are part of me. So how about if we just keep our 'stupid' jokes out of our relationship? Enough chit chat. Let's find that wire closet and see what's going on! Can you handle a soldering iron?"

Still groggy, David struggles to walk through the halls. He eventually finds the wire closet at the very end of an isolated hallway. Opening the door, he feels a blast of frigid Arctic wind. The small observation window has been shattered by the storm. The wire rack is covered with drifts of still-blowing snow.

He has no shovel to remove it, so he scoops out the snow with his hands. Then, he discovers the wire mounting rack has nearly been torn off the wall. All the solid copper wires were sheared off their electrical terminals by the wind's violent shaking.

In the dimly lit room, he takes off his gloves to feel

where to reattach the wires. He barely connects some that appear to be the most important, but they instantly break, as the mounting rack is still shaking from the wind streaming through the open window. He makes several attempts to salvage the wires, but they break every time. David knows then that they are too short from all the breaking, and too brittle from the numbing cold, to be repaired any further.

Melvin repeats, "Wire."

David, angry at having no success, shouts back, "I know, Melvin, I know! The wires are too cold, too short and too brittle."

Melvin then calls out to David, "Flexible."

Learning to trust more of Melvin's one-word advice, David realizes flexible wire will move with the wind and can be stretched. But where is he going to find such wire?

"Lamp," Melvin speaks into his mind.

David slams the door shut against the still-howling wind. Still weak and half crawling, he searches every room. All of the main lighting is fluorescent bars, but he finds tiny lamps in the lounge area. Ripping the wires out by hand, he makes his way back to the wire room. He opens the door, only to find the wind has caused the snow to drift back over the wire terminals.

Once again, David searches through accumulating snow to uncover the hanging wire rack and search for the correct broken telephone wires. Even in his half-frozen, delirious mind, he knows that to safeguard the nation against enemy attack he has to repair this most critical link. It is the heart of the communication system between the radar dome and the base camp below.

The room is almost pitch black, so David has to force his bare, numb hands to work from memory. Having no wire strippers, he uses his teeth to tear off the insulation. With the precious few pieces of lamp cord, he patches the critical wires. He then scoops the constantly drifting snow away from the door and closes it securely against the howling wind. Still not believing in such simple miracles, but too weak to doubt it, he turns around and opens the closet door one more time, praying to see the dangling, lifesaving lamp cords still alive and working.

To my amazement and joy, our miracle lamp wires are still attached, in spite of all the remaining twisting and turning caused by Mother Nature's wrath.

Exhausted, I stumble slowly down the hall to our phone, my one hope for rescue. I anxiously await the next lifesaving ring, praying that it is real, and not one of Melvin's tricks to get my attention. As I sit there my brain awakens a little more and it finally dawns on me not to just wait for a call from below to me, but to call down to them. Hopefully my friends are still alive in that warm, quiet oasis I called home so many days, maybe even weeks, ago. Actual time is lost to me right now.

SEARCHING FOR THE GOOD WAR

A Savior's Rescue

Before I can make that critical call down below, the phone rings. I know when angels call upon us we may hear the sound of their beautiful harps. Since it's not harps I hear, I finally believe I'm not really dead yet. It may not be harps, but this ringing sound from Mr. Bell's invention is just as beautiful to me, right about now. Out of the corner of my eye, I see that marvelous beacon of light flashing, just for me, so I know this call of survival *must* be real. Just in case the phone is much colder than I would like, I quickly grab a rag on the floor and put the receiver close to, but not on, my ear.

Not being able to say any words in days, not even to myself, I force my voice to say that magic word of greeting, "Hello?"

It's Eddie. He says, or is it shouting, into my still dull ears? "David, are you alive?" I realize this true friend cares for my health and know he doesn't realize how dumb his question is. I cannot say "hello" if I am dead. His deep concern for me on my first day, and again now, I will never forget.

After I assure him I am actually alive, he tells me things have been bad down below during the storm, but he knows not as terrible as it must be high up here in the very eye of the storm. He knows that, being on top of the mountain, I did not have the side of this giant mountain as a windbreaker to protect me as they did down below.

He now shouts very loudly, probably thinking that even if the phone lines fail, I could still hear him. He says he is coming for me with the Weasel, which has had some problems, but he thinks can make it. He also tells me that he is bringing up not one, but two, relief people. One is a repair technician who will try to resurrect a few more phone and Teletype connections and fix the window. The other is someone who insists on coming to my aid, even though he is still a little ill.

I know my constant savior, Eddie, must be bringing back my site supervisor and good friend, Lee. I hope he is well again. I tell Eddie to have the technician bring up a lot more lamp wire and to remember to turn the transmitter's cooling pump back on. I know Eddie really doesn't understand what I mean, and definitely thinks I really have lost my marbles about now.

He pauses and then says, "Okay, David."

Eddie warns me not to get too anxious about waiting. He is not sure how long it will take since the snow and drifts are very deep across our fragile mountain road. I thank him from the bottom of my heart and I also thank him again for saving me from that very angry Caribou on my first day.

He replies, "That's okay, David, but let's just skip doing that again, for a while." Mainly for my peace of mind, he repeats what he said about their being here as soon as possible.

With a sigh of relief, in a forced casual manner, I tell him, "I'll see you later, Eddie," and hang up.

I look around and can't believe the mess I made with broken lamps on the floor. My survival tables shoved up against the open transmitter doors that provided me some warmth during the coldest nights. The remnants of scraps of whatever food, even that nauseous Caribou meat, I was able to scrounge these past days.

In my still half-dull condition, I don't remember smelling the bathroom toilet, probably because the water, and anything in it, is still frozen solid. Sorry, my good friends and rescuers, I would love to help clean it up when it finally thaws, but I've had about enough of this wild life in the Arctic, and more excitement than I ever want again.

At last, I'm going home to warmth and safety. I'll be happy and healthy again.

The Miracle

NORAD is still in its perpetual "wait and see" routine, preparing for the final Global Nuclear War that all pray will never come.

"General, it's over. The miracle you asked for finally came. The Cape site is back up and communicating with us, and our radar boys have eyes on the Russians again. They undoubtedly know it, too."

"Great news, Captain, but remember our orders. This loss of our national defense site, the Cape, never happened. We have all been told to wipe it from our memories. If it ever leaks out, it's a court martial, even accusations of treason for all of us, and you know what that means. What is the name again of that young man up there, who is probably the one we have most to thank for our miracle?"

"Evans. Yes, General, we certainly do have a great deal to thank him for. He undoubtedly saved so much more that just our lives."

"Well, Captain, I hope he has a great life ahead of him when he finally gets back home and can leave his Arctic Hell behind."

"General, it's a pity that because of all the secrecy, the world will never know of what he did for us and can never give him a proper 'Thank You.'"

"But, Captain, at least you and I know, and will remember him and what he did for us."

"Yes, we know, General. We know!"

Nanook

After my three-day ordeal, Eddie is finally successful at getting me down to the base camp. For days I collapse into a state of near-death unconsciousness trying to recover from extreme cold and near starvation. Dreaming, I believe I died as a failure and a coward on the mountain and left all those I love behind.

During my recovery, a spirit comes to me. To some he may appear to be from the future, but in reality he is from a world where time and space have no meaning. He mysteriously appears out of the winter mist and snow flurries, and he looks just like my friend Nanook. He already understands my battles of many years against demons and of my special abilities, inherited from my mother and many ancestors before her.

Nanook begins by speaking in a strange language I do not know, but that I subconsciously comprehend. "There will also be others to visit and test you," he informs me. "Some will be those you love and have loved. Others, for which you have carried a life of hatred, will seek your forgiveness. While you have been on your journey to discover your true self and your destiny, some you love have died, but you must continue to learn courage and wisdom from the things they taught you. For now, it is I who shall be your teacher of the trials of life and death, and finding Unconditional Love during your moments of rest."

Nanook tells me that all I will learn will be important, as I will become the long sought-after moral leader to those isolated with me in the lonely Arctic because of my inspiration, faith, and courage to survive. My fellow workers believe I am the strongest among us. I must be the one to lead them into hope of a brighter future in times of trouble.

Nanook instructs me in the understanding and uses of my subconscious mind. He tells me what I will learn is knowledge from his ancestors who came from Tibet hundreds of years before. This is not true, for I can neither believe nor comprehend the fact that these are mystical powers I already possess and that Nanook will help me discover them. With Nanook's help, though, I learn the secrets of: mind/body control, out-of-body travel, self-hypnosis, prophetic visions, and the art of photographic memory.

He then discloses ways to survive the frigid Arctic cold by sleeping buried under the snow, next to resting Husky dogs. The last lesson I learn is the proper building of a snowstorm shelter, known as an igloo. When Nanook's time with me is complete, he departs with his loving family of dogs, into the winter flurries from which he came.

His departing words are a fatherly message, "You have become a faithful student and friend. Teach others in need what you have learned of faith and hope in a better tomorrow. A job well done, my son, a job well done."

Spiritual Questions to Answer

Just as Nanook foretold, David soon has other visitors. He both feels and hears the presence of a strangely familiar voice, his first visitor.

"Do you remember me, Wayne? You were still very young, only five or so when I met and fell in love with your mother. About the only jobs available were in the service, so I joined the navy to help support her and your family. Unfortunately, World War Two was just around the corner. You might remember me as Steve. You always called me 'Dad.' I was so proud that you thought of me as a true part of your family. We didn't have much time to do all those father/son things, but you must know I loved all of you as if you were really mine by birth."

"Steve, I do remember seeing you now and then, especially when we would all go visit your mother and father who we thought of as our Uncle Carl and Aunt Sarah. I loved milking the cows and feeding the noisy chickens. Why did you leave us alone like my first father did?"

"Wayne, the president called us all to active duty. I was sent to a little island in the Pacific Ocean called Oahu. My job was to help warn the ships in Pearl Harbor in case of an enemy invasion. My team and I were stuck on top of the highest bump on the island which we jokingly called a mountain. We were called 'spotters.' There was an early kind of radar on another bump some place, but I guess none of the brass trusted it yet. So, there we were, on this bump with nothing but field glasses, binoculars, to hopefully detect the enemy nobody expected out at sea. After all, we were thousands of miles from nowhere with nothing but water between us. Nobody could fly that far and ships were so big you could see them way before they could land for invasion.

"December 7, 1941, the impossible happened. It seemed as if hundreds, maybe even thousands, of airplanes came out of nowhere, and they weren't ours.

The Japanese attacked Pearl Harbor and launched our country into the Second World War. My team and I were the first to see them off in the distance. We tried to call to the base with our alert, but it was Sunday. Anyone with authority was either at church or still asleep. The Japanese were coming straight at us. We had no defense. You can't knock down bombers with a simple rifle or even a dumb machine gun. We had a saying, 'First to know and first to go,' and it all became true. The rest is history. That's why I never came back to your mother and all you kids, but I really felt I did my best to 'protect all I loved.'"

Next, David's long-dead older brother, Donald, who was killed in the Korean War, comes to him. "Don, I was younger than you, but since I was alone so many times I looked up to you for strength and wisdom. When the sad day came, that you were slaughtered at War, I could actually feel your violent Death in my soul, over thousands of miles apart. Why and how did you die?"

"My loving brother, I still do not understand the 'why' in your question, except I knew in my heart I had to serve 'to protect all I loved.' The 'how' was during the final days of the Korean War. A peace agreement had been signed, but radio communication with the North Koreans was nearly impossible. It was my team's mission to take the peace agreement to the enemy troops in writing. Not knowing hostilities were over, as we approached with a white flag, a North Korean sniper had a perfect target in his sights, me. With the last shot I never heard, and a silent death, the War was finally over."

"So, Don, you were no longer fighting War, but a true messenger of peace? Life is not fair."

"No, it isn't, but through Steve's and my death, we were doing what we had to do to protect all of you."

"Don, I know you never had a chance to instruct me in music, but I learned to play the harmonica like you did when you were overseas. You never had a chance to hear me, but I did it for you."

"I know, and am very proud of you to carry on with my music. I believe in you. Believe in yourself and all you may do to make the world a better place. I have always loved you, little brother."

Soon comes a spiritual message from David's loving grandmother who, upon his leaving her for the Arctic, had predicted she would not live to see his return. Her soul wishes to pass on to him her many years of courage and her wisdom of forgiveness. She especially wants him to forgive his father.

David's father then comes to him seeking forgiveness. David cannot reject his own father's plea for the same morsel of forgiveness he seeks for himself for causing George's death. But, that does not mean the process will be easy.

At first his father speaks only in riddles, "A man's

got to do what a man's got to do" (from John Wayne's character in *Stagecoach*). He then tells his son how his name was chosen at birth.

"Wayne is not an uncommon name, yet it was not one given to many children in 1935, when names were chosen for their exotic ring. Your mother and I had chosen 'Wayne' in honor of the man who, on and off the silver screen, exemplified the Strength and Courage to go on against all odds during those darkest days of the Great Depression and the ensuing War. It was our hope that our Wayne would someday develop the same Courage and beliefs shown to a struggling nation as by our hero, John Wayne."

"You sound like you were a caring man. So, why did you desert your family in the time of our greatest need, especially of your love?"

"It was *because* of my great love for all of you that I had to leave you alone to survive without a father."

Searching for understanding, David shouts at his father, "That makes no sense!!"

"Wayne, the Depression was a terrible time for families to stay together. There were so few jobs for so many in need, yet a father was expected to find some way to support his family. When I did find work, what I could earn was far less than what all of you had to have for even basic food and shelter. Our president knew this and started a program to help mothers with children survive through these worst of times, if left alone. If I stayed with you, you might have starved. With me gone, the government would provide you food and a place to live. I prayed and found the answer in the Good Book. 'There is no greater love than to give one's life to save all he loves.' I had to leave so you could live.

"I pray, my son, that you will find enough love in your heart to forgive me and, someday, once again, honor me by using the name I gave you at birth, 'Wayne.'"

With his training from Nanook and his other spiritual visitors behind him, David has a greater understanding of the visions and voices he has encountered since birth. He continues to discover more secrets of the Arctic, as he will need all the wisdom he has learned to battle the Demon of Death, very soon, and very alone.

Killer Stairs

David jerks awake and hollers "HELP! HELP!"

Eddie, who has been perched on a chair outside David's door since rescuing him from the mountain, rushes to his side. "What can I help you with?"

Still in a daze, David says, "No, not me, the young man outside the hallway door has fallen down the stairs outside and is freezing to death."

"No, David, that's just you remembering your terrible three-day storm."

David strains to whisper, "Go see."

Eddie believes David is hallucinating and hesitates to leave him alone. But, after covering him again with a blanket, Eddie does as David asks and investigates while David falls back into a deep sleep. The next day he finally wakes, but feels very weak, dehydrated, and hungry. Eddie hears him stirring and opens the door. David is sitting on the edge of the bed, still bent over from weakness.

Becoming more conscious of his surroundings, David asks, "Is that you, Eddie?"

David struggles to remember the phone call on the mountain, when Eddie asked, "Are you alive?" but he can remember nothing about his rescue. He only remembers the worst possible storm, the cold, and the pending destruction of his communications building.

"How long was I out?"

"Four days," Eddie replies.

"Where have you been?"

"Sitting outside your room in a lounge chair."

"I am hungrier than a Polar Bear. Did you get anything to eat out there?"

"Cookie kept bringing me something and never let up on telling me to go back to my room and get some sleep. All I said was no way, no how until David is fully awake. He needs me."

David asks about the frozen man.

"He is being flown to Kotzebue for treatment," Eddie

says. "How did you know?"

"I heard him calling for help."

Puzzled, Eddie says, "That's impossible. This place is like a World War Two bunker and the door outside to the stairs is at the other end of the hall."

David shrugs, "Well, that may be, but I didn't just hear him; I *felt* him freezing to death, just as I was myself up there on the mountain. Nanook told me I would feel the pain of others in trouble."

"Well, little brother, I know you always had feelings for people in trouble, but I think you might have just saved that young fella's life. Once we are off this mountain for good and I get to be an old man I hope you are around to take care of me when I need help, David."

"I don't know how to thank you, Eddie."

"Enough said. You would do the same for me, friend."

At David's prodding, Eddie goes for some well-deserved Cookie food. He soon returns, still chewing on something, "Well, did you have a great meal?"

"Yep, especially that extra piece of chocolate cake. Cookie felt sympathy for me after all these days. I saved you a piece, but you can't have it until you can come to the dining room and have a real meal."

"Eddie, tell me about the storm down here."

"You know, an Arctic storm comes and then goes just as fast. We mostly got nothing from the storm here, but we knew it might have blown you away, especially when we didn't hear from you for days. You know, you threw me for a loop on that lamp cord you told us to bring when we came up to get you. I knew that was a pretty fast trick you pulled to get us talking together and the radar boys telling us again what might be going on with those Russians."

"How much new snow since then?" David asks.

"None."

"Well, Eddie, do me a big favor, as crazy as it sounds. Go around the building and look outside my window, and tell me if something strange is out there."

"Okay, you asked for it, David."

Eddie returns shortly, and knocks on the door as he enters. "No such thing," he says in bewilderment.

"Well?"

First mumbling, and then a little louder, "Snow sled tracks, but that ain't all. The tracks just barely sank into the snow, kind of like there wasn't even a person sitting on it. And the craziest darned thing is that there were no dog tracks."

David looks at Eddie and grins.

"What the heck is going on?" Eddie asks, somewhat angry.

"You wouldn't believe me if I told you."

"Yes, I will, but only after two or three beers. I'll get the beers, and I know Cookie could rustle up some food for you, too."

"I'll eat anything except that damn Caribou meat!"

Battling Walrus

After surviving a death-defying time in the Arctic, on a day off, I'm taking a Sunday stroll along a desolate beach. I'm trying to relax and remember that I will be going home soon and will be with my precious Annie. *Will anyone really believe that I was here in this lonely place, so cold and frigid?* Sometimes I can't believe it myself, that I have had so many frightening experiences.

All of a sudden I hear a great commotion, and I can't believe my eyes. I spot two walruses fighting in the distance. I crouch low and duck behind a small hill. The walrus is a beautiful animal, but a ferocious fighter when sparse Arctic food or a prized mate is at stake. Soon the growling and cries of the battle are over, the wounded loser leaving behind a broken and bloody tusk.

Carefully picking it up, many thoughts go through my mind. I feel sorry for the Walrus that lost his bloody battle but, at the same time, his broken tusk is a wonderful souvenir that I can keep forever, never forgetting the many adventures—both good and bad—I have experienced, and how lucky I am to be going home soon.

I wonder, *What other close calls with beasts and dark nightmares still await me in this God-forsaken place?*

Polar Bear Lunch

Another day off and I get out my paints to create something I won't ever recognize. I had started painting shortly after my rescue from the mountain. I always wanted to paint as a child, and somehow the spiritual encounters I had during my recovery brought out a creative side of me I didn't know existed. Painting helps me stop thinking about battling Arctic Hurricanes, Caribou, and Walrus.

In the midst of my slapping paint on a canvas, my friend Eddie calls to tell me he needs a part delivered to him. He is up on the mountain having trouble with the Weasel. The problem is that the only truck available to go up the mountain has a little problem of overheating. Eddie tells me just to wait it out until the engine cools and then continue on. So, aware of the problem, I start up the mountain and, sure enough, there is engine trouble.

After waiting for a while to let the engine cool off, I have trouble starting it. Knowing that Eddie is expecting me, I need to let him know I will be delayed. A life survival shack, with a wired telephone, is not far away.

I have been told in my Arctic training that life shacks were placed along this narrow road in case anyone has trouble getting up the mountain. It is supplied with food and warmth necessary to survive until help arrives. Approaching the shack, normally surrounded by complete silence, terrifying growling noises penetrate my ears. Getting a little closer I see big footprints in the snow.

Immediately grabbing my camera, which I always have with me, and still being a fearlessly crazy young man, I take a picture of these giant footprints.

I quickly realize I had better get back to the truck, as the roaring is getting louder. No more investigations for me today. I realize I dropped my keys in my rush to get back to the protection of the truck. I start to panic, retracing my steps and looking for them. Going back towards that survival shack and checking into those giant footprints is *not* an option. *No, not in my pockets.* What a relief to see a tip of shiny metal in the snow just outside the truck door.

I don't see the Polar Bear, but he is still cussing a lot. He must be too busy trying to find a can opener to think about having me for lunch, and *not* as his guest. The truck starts and I am on my way again. You know, if that beast had shown up, you can be sure I would have taken his picture. After all, a person doesn't join a Polar Bear for lunch every day with himself on the menu as the main course. The roaring finally stops. Gunning the engine, I muster enough nerve to look behind me where there are more bear tracks.

Lucky for me, the bear is not coming back for me, but going the other way, dragging something rather bloody behind him. I guess I am not on his lunch menu today, but I feel sorry for whatever, or whoever, is soon to become that Polar Bear's dinner. I am so happy it's not me, at least not this time, but I will have to pass this way again tomorrow.

Eddie's Last Mission

Months later, with many other adventures behind him, David has successfully completed his year of duty and earned all the funds for his dreams to come true. By listening to those of great wisdom who came to visit him in his time of confusion, he learned many more hidden secrets of the Arctic world and discovered his own true self. He now possesses the knowledge of how to control his fears and call upon the light of his heart for strength.

David has fought many real and imagined battles, and believes he has come to terms with his guilt. He feels he has finally earned the gift of Eternal Love with Annie. David is packed and ready for his flight back to the real world when his good friend, Eddie, taps on the door.

"Come on in, Eddie." After a solid year together, David knows Eddie's distinctive knock well.

"Hey, short timer, need any help?"

"No, but thanks for asking."

Eddie has also served about a year and is scheduled to leave just one day after David. "Yeah, you get to fly the coop today, and I'm stuck with one more job. The boss wants me to take my Weasel to the mountaintop site for some early winter testing. You could call it my last impossible mission. Hey, that's got a nice ring to it. Maybe someday, since you've been the brainy guy around here, you can write some exciting stories about all the crap we have been through together.

"With all the Polar Bears, Caribou and Walruses we had to live with up here, you can tell everybody about the one beast we did *not* have to battle. That big, furry, Abominable Snowman. I remember when you got shook up early one morning with all that loud booming noise and believed the Russians had really come over the pole and started to bomb us. When you went out to investigate, what did you find?"

"Okay, Eddie, it wasn't the noise from exploding bombs, but it *was* Mother Nature slamming giant wedges of Arctic ice onto the beach. That ice almost ran over some of our smaller buildings."

"Yeah, Dave, you even took one of your pictures standing on a big slab of ice just to prove it all really happened when you finally get back home to Annie, someday, pretty soon now."

After sharing more stories of their times of danger and joy together, Eddie tells David, "Well, enough of this sob stuff. Give that Annie of yours a big kiss for me. Bye for now, little brother."

Waving one last time, he shuts the door. Then, Eddie opens the door again, just a crack—the last time he would ever do so—and whispers, "To be eternally free of your guilt and fears, you must discover the courage you have always had, and you will find the truth, the reason for your existence. Believe in yourself, and those who watch over you and believe in you. The truth will set you free."

David is speechless. Over the past year together, he has never heard his good friend, of a plain and humble background speak such words of wisdom.

Eddie then speaks his last, "Somewhere in time and space we will meet again, for I will always be your friend, Wayne."

Then he quietly shuts the door. David is stunned. *Wayne? But no one up here knows my first name.*

Day 455

David does not yet know his sacrifice of three days in frozen hell turned the world away from the death of hated War towards the seeds of lasting peace. His bags are packed, and before his flight Cookie escorts him to the dining room for one last meal on the Cape. But the only food David *really* wants is back home with Annie, tasting her precious lips once again.

As they enter the dining room, the captain calls, "Attention!"

It is a celebration held in secret. Only a few were invited to attend, and they are bound to never disclose it ever even happened. But, as his spiritual father, I must tell you of his boundless service to his country and to the world, for he is my special son of whom I am forever proud.

The entire room stands up, raises their glasses and shouts, "To the man who stopped a Nuclear War!" Then everyone applauds while David stands there looking bewildered.

Cookie explains, "By monitoring the Russians' radio traffic, talking about your weakening signal problems during that three-day storm, our counter-intelligence group discovered the Russians gave up any idea of a first-strike invasion onto your site. They backed off because you plugged any possible holes in our Alaska National Defense Communication System by keeping your signal alive, in spite of your three days alone and freezing."

"Any one of you would have done the same thing."

"We don't think so, David, just you," the captain assures him. "That three-day storm was bad enough down here, but we couldn't know how terrible it was up on top. After the second day of getting absolutely no communication of any kind from you and the radar boys, some of the newer fellows, who don't know you well, thought you had been bought off by the Russians."

"You mean you thought I was a spy!?"

Blushing from embarrassment at their mistake, Cookie interjects, "When Eddie went up to get you on the third day and told us just how badly the building had been torn apart and saw the lamp cord you used to restore our vital communication system, he was overwhelmed. On behalf of all those who shamed your reputation by doubting your allegiance to your country, I apologize."

"Enough," says Captain. "Those terrible days are over for all of us. We are still alive. No invasion."

Cookie takes a strangely familiar piece of paper out of his pocket. He signs it with the date and time, just as the dining room clock strikes exactly 12 noon. All of David's friends applaud him again for a job well done. Exactly to the very minute, David's 15 lonely months—455 days away from Annie on his Arctic mission—are finally ended.

Cookie tells David, "You have earned every penny, and more, for doing your job for the past year in this hell hole. In fact, on your way back, stop by our government headquarters in Anchorage and pick up your bonus, a very sizable bonus. Oh, by the way, they want you to take charge of the construction of a completely new Alaskan national defense radar system starting immediately. Of course, you would be away from home again for over a year. Think about it—very hard—but not too long."

David then realizes Cookie is much more than "just" a cook.

What has Cookie seen in David, and liked, that even David himself didn't realize yet? Maybe Cookie knows that if anyone could handle the worst possible conditions and still protect his country, David could, as he did for those three days, even though he was near death.

The joy of David's last meal with his friends for the past

year is interrupted by an announcement that the first winter storm is starting to blow in from the Arctic Ocean. David knows from experience just how unexpected and unpredictable the first storm of the winter season can be. These storms may start moderate, but then explode into Arctic Hurricanes. The snow always begins on the top of the mountain and works its way down, which is why Eddie was chosen to go up there to check out the new snow tracks on the Weasel.

The loudspeaker announces David's plane for home has taken off from Kotzebue village on schedule. David prays the storm is not so bad that the pilot would have to abort his attempt to reach the Cape.

Cookie tells David, "You know, this early in the winter season it happens all the time. These Arctic bush pilots can fly in anything. Even tundra mush soup. As he gets closer, he'll be calling in any minute for landing instructions. It will work out just fine. Come on. Let's eat. It's your favorite food, David, Caribou."

Upon hearing this, David almost gags, "The only food I had to eat during those three days of nightmares alone on the mountain during that winter hurricane was frozen Caribou meat. For breakfast, lunch, and dinner. After the first day, I could eat no more. I believed, with one hundred twenty-five-miles-an-hour winds at ninety-five below zero, I would certainly freeze to death long before I starved."

Realizing David's emotional reaction to his not-so-funny joke, Cookie apologizes, "Only kidding, David. Sorry," and brings David his real last meal on the Cape.

David smiles, "It looks and smells great, Cookie."

Love or Friendship

There is no time to eat. The captain of the base re-enters and calls, "Attention!"

This time, he is not greeted with happiness and cheers. He announces an explosion and fire have just occurred on the mountaintop.

"Who's hurt?" I ask, my voice cracking as I tell myself I probably already know.

"Eddie," is the captain's single reply, his eyes downcast.

I jump up shouting, "I must go for him!"

The captain says, "Evans, I know he has become a good friend but your year here is up today. Your plane to take you back home may be landing any minute now. I have two others going back with you who also deserve to go home, so I can't hold up the plane until you get back down." The Captain continues, "Eddie's many other friends are desperately searching for ways to rescue him in this storm. Eddie is doing what he loves with his crazy Weasel. He is doing what he feels is his duty. Your duty, while here in the Arctic, was to help save your country in times of War. It's over for you. Go home to your loved ones, now. That's an order."

"Sorry, Captain, I know you want to help me. I respect you, but I don't need to follow your orders anymore. As you just said, my tour is over."

The Captain pleads, "With the Arctic weather changing so fast, Evans, it may be days, possibly weeks, before another plane can make it back for you. You can't miss this one."

"You're right, Captain, but in spite of the storm, I'm going up top to get my friend Eddie first. He needs me right now. I know Annie will wait for me and understand what I must do. This is my second chance to save a friend. I failed my first one when he needed me the most. I must not fail again." I turn and run to my room for my Arctic gear.

At the motor pool, I see Eddie's fellow mechanic and friend, Bob. "Where's the other Weasel?" I demand.

"It's down for repairs."

Normally known as Mr. Cool, I feel desperate to help Eddie. My physical being feels every instant of Eddie's final struggle to survive. The roar of the other motor vehicles' engines being tested and tuned up for winter is not helping my mood at all.

"What bucket of bolts *do* you have that at least runs and is gassed up?"

"Just the boom truck, but it doesn't have any tire chains on yet, and may be a sliding death trap up there without them in this freezing snow."

My mind can no longer bear mirroring Eddie's suffering. I must put my dream of a new life and hope for true love behind me for now. I command my total self—mind, body, and soul—go and save my friend.

I cry out to my Eternal Love, "Forgive me, Annie, for what I have to do!"

Again, Bob warns me of the ever-growing storm and danger on the icy mountaintop, but I remember what was taught by the greatest teacher of self-sacrifice over 2,000 years ago, *There is no greater love than to give one's life for a friend.* "Forget the lousy chains. For Eddie, I'll take the damn truck!!!"

Rescuing Eddie

David barrels up the narrow mountain road to Eddie. Without even seeing the radio site, a vision of the truth flashes in David's mind—the violent explosion and flames engulfing Eddie's Weasel, the noxious fumes of leaking gasoline, the screams from Eddie's scorched throat, and the agonizing pain of Eddie's soul crying for deliverance. As Nanook predicted, the stage is set for David's final battle in his perpetual search for forgiveness, the cleansing of his body and mind from his many years of guilt. This would be his final battle with WAR. This is the very moment for which both Eddie and David were born, and possibly to die.

As he corners the last mountain bend, David sees Eddie's Weasel is actually burning. His vision was insight into what is really happening to Eddie. David vows he will not give up until he saves his friend.

David knows he will have to drive across the ice

against strong crosswinds to reach Eddie, but since the boom truck has no tire chains for gripping he could be blown off the mountain to his own death. The closer David gets to the top, the stronger the wind blows, blowing the truck sideways across the narrow mountain road. David tries to drive crosswise against the wind, as in a sailboat. Whenever he stops, the tires stop sliding. When he tries to move slowly forward, the tires slip and the truck slides again. He is stuck.

Determined he will reach his friend, David revs the engine, completely flooring the gas pedal. The wheels spin, but cause enough friction to burn through the thin layer of ice under them. It is just enough of a break in the ice for him to gain traction.

David finally reaches the top. In an attempt to stop the truck, he tries to turn it broadside to the ever-growing wind, which causes him to slide even more. The wind pushes the huge truck across the ice, right into the side of the communication building, sealing the access door needed to remove Eddie. On a stretcher, Eddie will not fit through the small observation windows, the only other way out.

David shouts to the two men on duty, "Climb out and help me push this damn truck away from the door!"

After clearing the door, David realizes Eddie cannot sit up in the passenger seat, but the truck's storage area is loaded with maintenance equipment. The stretcher won't fit, and the equipment is too heavy to carry into the building to make room for Eddie.

Over the howling wind, David shouts, "Just push all this junk out of the truck onto the ice ground and slide it out of the way!"

As carefully as possible, David and Eddie's other friends put the stretcher with Eddie in the truck and force the doors shut against the battling wind. David then begins his treacherous journey to get Eddie to medical attention at the base camp below. As difficult and dangerous as it was to drive up the sloping ice, going downhill will be far worse. The downward slope is a twisting snake of ever-slippery ice. The growing Arctic wind could force them both to the very edges of the narrow road, and plunge them thousands of feet below to their deaths.

Charging Beasts

David turns the last icy corner to what should have been a safer road, one protected from the storm by the height of the mountain. Instead of a safe, snow-free path to the base camp and Eddie's medical aid, he is greeted by the sight of three giant Caribou charging towards him, blocking the narrow road of his only escape. David believes the one in the middle is the same glassy-eyed beast he had met on his first day at the Cape, now back to even up the score. This time he brought his whole smelly gang with him.

David desperately calls for help from Michael, Melvin, Nanook, and even George, but hears only the thunder of pounding hoofs.

Never one to miss an opportunity to torture his enemy, WAR snarls, "See, David? All your so-called friends have deserted you in our final battle for your soul. Admit it. You are truly guilty of your friend George's murder by not saving him. Your game of survival is over. You cannot keep these beasts from pushing you to your death."

Melvin speaks up and reminds David, "Fear saves!"

David recalls Nanook's words to him during his recovery from unconsciousness, "You cannot eliminate fear, but you can control it. Turn it around so your enemies fear you more than you fear them."

"Hook, muffler, horn, and buck are your tools of fear," Melvin says.

David has always called this strange truck a monster. Now he has to turn it into a giant one so fearful as to stop the inevitable Caribou stampede.

With draining courage, he shouts "How?"

Unconditional Love

Searching his pocket for one last touch of her love for him, David feels the letter he had received from Annie just that morning.

"Dear love of my life, our time of loneliness and sorrow is at last over. No more letters, tapes, or calls full of lies to protect me from the truth of your world of death. You are healed from your past of shame, guilt and fear. You no longer need to hide them from others behind the mask of David.

You must come home to me as you were when we first met on that magical night, when you held me so very close as we danced. I so need you to come back to me as you were, my Soldier Boy, Wayne. Not next year, not next week, not tomorrow, but now, my darling. Now."

With renewed strength and determination, David screams, "No! Not in this Frozen Hell. No! Not after all the crap we have been through together. To die now? Not in this place. Not at this time."

He guns the engine with the roar of the missing muffler, lowers and violently swings the hoisting hook, blasts the bullhorn, and bucks the monstrous beast back and forth, primed to attack. He guns the engine again and pops the clutch, sending clouds of dust and early winter snow into the heavens.

He fixes his gaze on the glassy eyes of that giant Caribou, turns his unbelievable fear toward his enemy, and stops their charge. They turn around and race to get out of the way of the monster racing to push them out of the way and off the mountain.

David then sees over 20 more Caribou coming up the narrow road behind the first three and, gunning the engine even more, he takes on the entire herd in battle, three Caribou at a time. They, too, run from David's monster of a truck.

David knows it is true, "Fear *can* save" and "Unconditional Love can win over Fear."

With the road finally clear of wild beasts, David races Eddie to the medics. They tell him they will take care of Eddie, and for him to get on the plane that has just landed after being delayed by the storm.

David rushes to the airstrip, where he sees a "true" airplane with two beautiful, shiny engines ready to restart. It is not the bucket of bolts that almost took his life as it crashed on the Cape beach so many lonely months ago. His baggage is already on board, loaded by the other two agents waving him on, as they are anxious to get home.

Even in his excitement over returning to Annie, David deeply worries about Eddie who, for a solid year, became not just a friend, but his second best friend. Even a brother, as it was with George. He remembers their times of both joy and fear. He especially feels he could never thank Eddie enough for when, time and time again, Eddie came to rescue him, to truly save him. He knows he will never forget his eternal friend, Edward.

The Return to Yesterday

I look back one last time at the base camp. The days of almost 24-hour sun are giving way to the days of almost 24 hours of pitch black, frigid winter, and I realize I will not see it ever again. After a solid year in isolation here, thousands of miles from modern civilization, my airplane of deliverance begins to roar with the mighty power of those two magnificent engines. Unlike the one-engine bucket of bolts that limped its way onto the beach runway so many long months ago, this angel of heavenly flight is still right side up.

The plane begins its smooth roll and then lifts me effortlessly towards a heaven of long-forgotten happiness. The pilot loops back over the Arctic Ocean and slowly passes the dining room windows. This time, not to shield us from the treacherous Arctic winds, but to let us wave one last farewell to our friends who wish they were with us, on their way back home. Gaining altitude, he makes one more pass over our little shacks tied together with the fragile threads of companionship, so desperately needed in this land of perpetual loneliness. Off in the distance is the narrow road to the mountain that holds the memories of so many exciting adventures that threatened my very survival.

One more turn, and the Arctic Ocean is on my right. As Eddie told me, I now know we are headed south, forever south. Now a mile high, we are level with the top of the mountain where the bright white radar dome glows in the early fall sunlight. Behind it are the giant, seven-story antennas and my fragile radio shack, recently repaired after the three-day storm that nearly took my life. I almost died in a world of Fear and Hate, but then I was reborn into one with George's Courage and Annie's Unconditional Love.

As the engines purr with the delight of taking us back to our loved ones, we all three sit in silence. Maybe we are in shock of the reality that home is only a few thousand miles and a very few days before us. After a solid year and a half in this sad world beyond our lives of yesterday, these new lives of deliverance seem only minutes away.

A restless nap, and soon Kotzebue is on the horizon. The pilot tells us our new plane can travel 1,000 miles, directly to Nome, so we will not be landing here. I look and see the tree line that signifies life off in the distance. They may be stubby scrubs, but they look tall and green to me after all that soggy, Arctic tundra.

I feel the temperature rising a few degrees now and then as we travel further south to warmer weather. Soon the last radio call is heard. Then, the landing approach and the smooth, almost silent touchdown. After we coast to a stop, I ask the pilot if I have time to visit some old friends in town.

He answers, "Sure. We will be here about two hours.

It stays daylight for a number of extra hours this time of year, so we should make it to Anchorage before dark. Have a good visit."

I am anxious to see my old friend Nanook and his wife. I want to thank her again for her beautiful wedding dolls and reminisce about the first time we met a year ago. But, I have a strange feeling of sadness overtaking me. Soon, I come to the corner where I first saw the little shop with water hoses going inside from the edge of wooden sidewalks. Anxious to shake hands and hug them, and to answer any questions they may have about my adventures at the Cape, I am shocked at what I see. No water hose. No open door. No smiling, loving greetings. Nothing but wooden boards blocking my entrance to fond memories of a year ago.

I look around, trying to find someone to answer my sad questions. What happened to them? Where are my friends? Then I realize they lived a hard life in northern

Alaska, and maybe our first meeting of joy and their final wave to me was their last. Saddened by what I find of their now empty store, and emotional as to how short life's friendships can be, I begin to wonder if Nanook's death created a loving spirit, and whether it could be the same Nanook who came to me in the days I spent recovering from that terrible snowstorm. Was he my teacher of Forgiveness, Love, and Secrets of the Arctic I needed to survive my hatred of WAR? I cannot say for sure, but believe we all have a destiny and maybe he found his by helping me.

I slowly walk back to the waiting plane with a sad heart, but with fond memories of this loving couple who had boundless wisdom and words of love.

Anchorage, Money, Memories, and Regrets

We are now on our last leg of our journey to Anchorage. I see the trees getting taller, the ground getting greener, and the temperature getting warmer. It even feels hot to me after living in an Arctic ice box for a year. I again see the lake where I visited the family living in the wilderness to escape the anticipated bombing of populated areas such as Anchorage. I believe I see one of the many villages we explored during our training. Even at a distance I can see the bright colors of the freshly painted buildings that house the dead glistening in the bright August sun overhead.

In my first summer of training, I was proud to be part of the celebration when Alaska became the 49th state. Long gone are the thousands of visitors, members of the press, and television reporters. While I was up in the Arctic playing with Caribou, Walrus and Polar Bears,

Hawaii became the 50ᵗʰ state. Those glorious 49-star flags only flew for a few months. Those that are left are now just part of somebody's museum collection. Life in the limelight is fleeting, even for a state.

Closer to Anchorage, as we approach for a landing, I see that the streets, the shops, and the churches are still as I remember, but the people are fewer and farther between. Next we fly over the apartment complex where Peggy, Frank, Sue, and all the other members of our volleyball team played. It was where all of us recruits lived during our three-month training, and while waiting for our security clearances. The complex also housed all of the military who were part of the training complex and local air force base, including Sue's father and family. Suddenly, my eye catches something strangely familiar, but mostly different—the classified training complex. Now, it is almost naked compared to all the constant activity of just a year ago.

Our landing at the Anchorage airport is soft, almost silent, and even relaxing after a full day of my never ending journey south, far away from my life in the Arctic. I'm scheduled to fly to my next stop, Seattle, the next morning, so I might as well use the extra daylight to my advantage. With my overnight bag in hand, I rent a car. As Cookie told me to do, I first stop at the headquarters of the hush-hush government group that hired me so many months ago.

Spies, Spies, and More Spies

As I walk in, the company manager, I think, says, "Welcome back, Wayne, or do you go by David now?"

"Wayne is how you hired me."

"Good. That's how we made out the cashier's check for all the great work you did at the Cape and for completing your mission. You're quite a celebrity to many up there, especially Cookie. As he told you, we also have a sizable bonus check for you. You have certainly earned it as our reports on the enemy's Bering Sea activity shows."

"Thanks."

"No, we thank you. Now, down to business. As Cookie told you, we are building a new Alaska defense long-range radar and communication system, and he recommended you to head up one of the technical operations. We would be proud to have you, but you realize you would be up here for another year or so. What do you think?"

"I think it's a fantastic opportunity and I know the money would be great, but..."

"Yes, but what?"

"I already have another life waiting for me back home, with a fine young lady to marry, college, a good job—I hope—and even children someday, if that radiation exposure I took lets me be a father."

"Yes, we have a report on that, and hope that part of your dream works out well for you, too. If that's your decision, we understand, but we will miss you and your talents. I know you will do fine in your new studies.

"I have something extra for you. It's not much for all your valuable accomplishments in Alaska, especially at the Cape. It may be just a piece of paper to most, but when you display it on a wall in your new home with your Annie, think of it as a unique medal your grateful country has awarded you, a special son, in which it is extremely proud."

The paper he hands me reads:

Certificate of Appreciation

Wayne W. Evans

This testimonial is awarded for having faithfully, loyally and ably performed his assignment as Station Technician on the White Alice Communications System within the Boundaries of Alaska on a project Vital to the Defense of North America.

In witness whereof we have here to set our hand and seal

This 6th day of August, 1960

Federal Electric Corporation Operation and Maintenance Contractors to the United States Air Force for the White Alice Communications System

"Sir. This is quite an honor. Thank you. How *is* the new National Defense Radar and Communications System coming along?"

"You know I can't tell you that now, but I can tell you it won't be long before you won't need to worry about 'spilling the beans' concerning all the technology you learned about and protected up here, because it will soon be obsolete."

"So it is okay if I put this nice Certificate of Appreciation on a wall back home?"

"Certainly. It just says, Station Technician. But you can even tell your family what you really were up here. 'An Arctic Secret Agent Battling Lies, Spies, and Wild Beasts,' as you put it, but don't be surprised if nobody believes you. Thank you for all your hard work in protecting our country. We wish you and your waiting loved one all the happiness in the world. You both deserve it."

"Oh, my flight home is not until tomorrow. I would like to visit the training site tonight."

"Sure, Wayne. Go right ahead. You certainly know where it is."

"Thank you, but won't I need a password to get through the gate?"

"Not anymore. Just walk right in and have some fond memories."

"I'm still a little bewildered by all this spy stuff, but thanks again."

"Let me shake your hand again for a job well done, Wayne, and don't lose those checks.

"Yes, sir."

He then salutes me. I salute him back.

Journey into All My Yesterdays

While there is some daylight left, I decide to visit my former training headquarters. A top secret facility during my training, the gates were always locked and attended to by special military police. As I approach, though, I see the gates are swung wide open and no one is in sight. Only a few vehicles, mainly some old delivery trucks and a training Weasel, are haphazardly scattered around the grounds. Most of the curved roof Quonset huts left over from World War Two have been removed. The highly classified technology and Arctic training buildings exist no more. I do see the main office and auditorium building still standing. I try the front door and surprisingly it opens with barely a touch of my somewhat quivering hand.

Visions of what I may no longer see make me nervous as I cautiously enter. The brown Kodiak and white Polar Bear hides are no longer displayed on the walls by the bar. The corner where Dr. Varian and I had our talk about television, radar, and his Klystron transmitting tubes, with their heat and radiation problems, is void of any tables or chairs. Gone is the laughter of graduation parties once held every three months as the newly trained agents moved on to their assigned sites and new students arrived.

It has all become obsolete and is being replaced by the newer, more powerful and secure radar and communication sites throughout the free world. Just as it was when the technology I had learned in the military was of little value in civilian life, what I have learned in the Arctic is also now obsolete. Yes, obsolete, as are all those who were trained to use it.

Only 24 and I, too, am obsolete—again. My only choice is to again move on to an even higher level of knowledge with additional schooling. Annie and I foresaw such setbacks in my career and had already made plans to earn further college credentials upon my return home.

With sunset now close at hand, and with no place to rest overnight, I take this last journey into my many yesterdays and visit the same apartment complex where I met and played volleyball with many close, though only temporary, friends. Fortunately, the main office is still open and the manager is working late. I enter and ask if there are any vacant rooms left for just one night.

She responds kindly, "Take your pick. With the training center shutting down, there are no more students, and even no instructors. So, as I said, take your pick."

"Do you have number 127 available? I lived there while training last year at this time."

"Oh, yeah. I think I remember you and your friends playing a lot of volleyball, and you didn't bother others with too much partying."

"We tried not to," I grin.

"The sheets are clean but may be a little dusty. Do you want me to change them?"

"No, don't bother. It's only for one night. I'll be leaving for the airport early tomorrow. It's warm out here to me so I'll just plop down on the blankets and doze off. It's been a very long day."

"Where are you coming in from?"

"The Cape, on the Arctic Ocean."

"Wow! Did those Russians bug you much?"

"I can't say."

"Oh, yeah, all that hush-hush stuff. I'm used to it from all of you fellas over the years. Well, have a good rest. Not much going on around here anymore, so I think I'll just go on home. Have a nice flight to wherever you're going tomorrow."

"Oh, how much for the room?"

"Nothing. You came up here to help keep us safe, so

it's the least I can do for you."

"That's very nice of you."

"That's okay. Just think of it as something from the good old days, when people cared about each other. Good night."

"You, too."

I move the car to the door of number 127. I could have parked just about anywhere, because there are almost no cars around. As I start to take my overnight bag inside, I look down to the end of the lot and think I recognize the apartment where Sue and her parents lived. A quick walk, and I'm there. A gentle knock on the door, and a young man opens it.

"Yeah?"

Using Sue's family name, I ask, "Is this the Sundstrum residence?"

"Never heard of 'em, and I've been living here almost a year now. They friends of yours?"

"Yes, they were. I mean, they are."

"Hope you find 'em."

"Oh, thanks anyway. Sorry to disturb you."

"That's okay. Night."

Back at my one-night apartment from my past, I unlock the creaking rusted front door for the last time. I know I will sleep very little, with both happy and sad memories of these same lonely rooms running through my mind. I can see again all the volleyball games and the explorations to strange, far north villages with new friends, especially Frank, Peggy, and Sue. I know Sue's rushing to me from her first plane on her first day as a new stewardess filled her with joy.

The next morning, just as when my year in the Arctic began, and my small plane to the endless north began to roll, I looked out the window. Instead of a last wave from my friends, I saw the sadness of Frank and Peggy holding Sue as she cried. This vision still haunts me the most. I pray our occasional evening walking and talking together helped her know she was not alone in her confused, young world. So many truly care for her.

So much for my return homecoming and memories of the Anchorage of long ago. Tomorrow is another day. I have a long way yet to go to finally be back home in Chicago. Being away for so very long, I hope my family there hasn't forgotten me, especially my Annie.

Believe in Your Dreams

During the year that David was away, Sue matured in many ways. She became the chief stewardess and gained knowledge of the times and gates assigned to all the airplanes arriving in and departing from Anchorage.

She is now flying in larger four-engine planes between Anchorage and Seattle. She knows about David's return flight from Nome to Anchorage, and when and where he will land. She is desperate to arrange her flights so she can be there to greet him and give him a loving hug just as she did after her very first flight over an endless year ago.

Through casual conversations with her father, a military security agent, she discovers a new radar system is being constructed at a secret site not too far from Anchorage. There is to be a top executive meeting at the new headquarters, but they all have to be flown in from Seattle in a rapid-turnaround red-eye flight.

This airplane and all its young crew have been secretly selected because they are known as the very best and can weather the long and strenuous double shift required to make the flight successful.

Precisely as David's plane is scheduled to take off from Nome to pick him up in Anchorage, Sue's plane is scheduled to take off for Seattle. There, they would pick up her special passengers, quickly refuel, and return to Anchorage by early the next morning.

Sue realizes her superiors have purposely picked her for this special mission, a journey that could make or break her career. Her mind tells her she must go, but her heart tells her she must stay so she can be with David at least a day, an hour, or even a minute, and at last show him how much she loves him before he leaves her, maybe forever.

Sue checks her flight schedules and believes that if all goes as planned she could make the round trip and land back in Anchorage and get to David's departing gate in time. She has visions of his holding her hand once again as she tells him what she could not say when he left her crying at the airport a year ago, "I love you so. Please don't leave me."

She knows David has plans to marry his Annie upon his return, but wants to believe that Annie has grown weary of waiting and found someone else to love. If so, Sue could have a life with David.

Her mind wanders, *You can stay with me now. You can get a job building this new radar site close to me. There are fine schools here where you can continue your dream of greater education. Peggy and Frank met here a year ago, fell in love and got married. Why can we not do the same?*

Sue is shocked out of her dream of a life with David, and finds herself at the special military airport outside Anchorage. With the flight crew already on board, but no passengers, Sue boards the plane, but struggles to believe in her dreams. *We can make the round trip and be back in time for me to be with you, David,* she assures herself.

Once in the air, the dark, long, and tiring night begins. They land safely in Seattle, quickly board the special passengers, and start their return flight to Anchorage.

This dream of mine must come true, even if I have to get out and push the plane faster myself. Hoping against hope, Sue wills time to stand still until she can be with David once again.

Looking at her watch, Sue thinks, *After all my struggles to get back here now, I have enough time. I know I can make it. I must make it.* She has yet to discover that "time stands still for no one."

Sue knows David's flight number, the time, the departing gate and even the exact seat next to a window that she picked for him so they may see each other and wave until the very last instant of time that she can be with him. Sue has been trained to help the passengers safely exit down the stairs before she leaves the plane herself. But, the window of time is quickly disappearing for her to run to David before he boards. So, as the plane lands, she declares an "emergency" and bolts past the descending passengers and rushes into the terminal.

Yes, his gate is number 20. Professional or not, if I run fast enough, I will make it to him with plenty of time to hug him as I first did so many months—no, years—ago. I pray he will hold me and caress me in return.

Down the main hall, a sharp turn, and then a long breathless run to David's gate, but David is not there! Nobody is waiting to board.

"Where is flight 8?" Sue shouts. A lone check out attendant says, "There was a luggage loading problem at Gate 20, so they moved Flight 8 to Gate 5."

"Oh no! All the way back to 5. I just passed Gate 5. Had I not blindly rushed so much, I could have seen him waiting, waiting for me. If he had only known I was desperately searching, I know he would have turned to see me coming to him."

Sue quickly turns and makes a mad dash down the hallway, all the way from Gate 20 back to Gate 5. Now, out of breath and only at Gate 10, the wind blows off her flight attendant cap, and she steps on it, crushing the pride of her achievement over the past year. She dares not stop to pick it up and brush it clean, losing precious seconds in her struggle to reach David in time.

Gates 9, 8, 7, 6.

Almost collapsing from exhaustion, Sue finally reaches Gate 5. "Flight 8?"

The boarding attendant is packing up her belongings, "Yes, they have just finished boarding and are about to leave."

SEARCHING FOR THE GOOD WAR

Sue pleads, "I *must* say goodbye to someone on that plane, to tell him I love him. I know the seat number. It won't take long."

"I'm sorry, miss. The stairs have already been pulled away and now the engines are starting. I can't let you on. I wish I could, but I can't."

"Can I go through the departing doors and out to the observation fence so I can at least wave goodbye?"

"Yes, that is the least I can do for you. When will you see him again?"

"Never!" Sue moans.

Sue searches for the window through which she prays David will see her waving and crying once again. This time, not with her friends Frank and Peggy holding her, but this time to suffer her sorrow and grief alone.

Sue sees the window where David is sitting as the plane backs out and turns to taxi to the runway. The glare of the early morning sun reflecting off the plane's windows blinds her. David cannot see out, for the sun's glare has blinded him, too. With the blinding sun, in his airtight plane, he cannot see Sue's final wave or hear her cries of a lost lover's pain.

As the plane turns further towards the departing runway, the glare on the plane windows begins to fade. Sue finds David's window again and searches for his smile, but because of David's mild Arctic snow blindness, she sees only the shade as he pulls it down against the still-damaging sun.

David's airplane of deliverance turns the last corner to the waiting runway. Sue knows he can no longer see or hear her, but every nerve in her body screams to him. In spite of those around her, Sue's voice joins the chorus of nerves "David, I love you! I have always loved you!"

While Sue is trying to hang on to David, he is reliving his sad journey back from the Cape just one day ago. Everything he knew and enjoyed during his three months in Anchorage is now gone, nothing but dying memories.

There was no one to greet me last night when I returned from that lonely year on the Cape. No Frank. No Peggy. No Sue. No laughing young stewardess rushing into my arms, desperately wanting me to feel how she is no longer a child. Now on this last leg of my journey to my real home, there are no friends to wave goodbye and no sad sight of Sue crying as she was when I left her for the Arctic one frightening year ago.

Of course, David does not know of Sue's struggle, running through the airport, just to be with him one last time, and how very close he was to being with her before he left. Yet, as his plane taxis further away from Sue, David feels her presence in his mind and speaks to her as a true friend.

Yes, Sue, at a different time, in a different place, we might have made a life together, but we have different dreams. You, of flying as a stewardess, and me of returning to my real home, marrying my Annie, going to college, and raising a family. I pray your life becomes a happy one, full of fulfilled dreams, and that at last you meet someone who can be a true soul mate of understanding, sometimes by just holding your hand with love.

Sue knows she will never be with David again, for he is on his last journey to return to his True Love after their Eternity apart. Sue's thoughts turn to Annie. She now feels a strange bonding with Annie and understands Annie's strength to believe that her and David's dream, formed so many years ago, will finally come true. From her heart of sorrow, Sue composes a letter in her mind to her new "friend."

Thank you, Annie, for sharing your David with me for just a very short time. Not his love, for that only exists for you, but his smile, his ability to understand others' struggles, and his belief in a better world where dreams like yours can come true.

He taught me to believe in myself, to grow from a child into a strong woman with the power to control my own destiny. Because of this power, I must now swallow my pride, release to you my forbidden love for him, and move on with my life. I, too, have always had a dream, one of flying, of seeing the beauty and feeling the love of the heavens. My dream is now coming true, and who is to say, maybe one day, on one of my journeys yet to come, I will meet another young man with a sparkle in his eyes, a loving smile, and a gentle hand. Who can tell? He may call me Susan, and I may call him Wayne. That's a nice name."

The Final Journey, Alone

My plane finally begins its ascent into the overcast sky above Anchorage. Yet, it is not like the dark, black days of the Arctic I left just hours ago. As my eyes try to see through the mist, sights of my recent past begin to disappear into the horizon. The training camp; apartment number 127; Peggy, Frank, and Sue, are all dissolving into nothingness.

My travels of thousands of miles ends as when I first arrived those many months—or was it years—ago... Alone. Now, though, my life's journey is played in reverse. My camera is no longer hanging around my neck waiting for that next exciting shot. No more attacking Caribou. No more photos with the snow-capped mountains of Alaska off in the distance. No more islands, or tiny villages and ships along the coast of Canada. These are images of my past that will soon be replaced with those of the new golden life waiting for me just over the horizon.

Something isn't right. *Why does my plane feel as if it is slowing down? It must be the head winds coming from the warmer south. But I cannot be late getting into Seattle. Somebody will be expecting me in Chicago.* The pilot confirms the plane will be a little late in landing at Seattle, but we will still be able to make our connecting flight for Chicago.

Soon comes the screech of the landing gear wheels, the agonizingly long taxi to the terminal, and the mad rush to the departing gate for my final flight back to Chicago. *I have my overnight bag with me, but what of the rest of my luggage, the wedding dolls given to me by my Nome friends?* As I frantically turn the last corner to my next gate, an announcement is made that the luggage for Chicago-bound passengers will be on the next flight, to be picked up later. *But how much later after I land? Will they still wait now, not just for me, but for my gifts, especially for Annie?*

Now at the gate and through the fence, I start up the stairs and am shocked at what I see. Four *giant* engines like nothing I have ever seen before. They are so large, in fact, that I don't know how the short, stubby wings can support them flying hundreds of miles an hour. I have read all about the new jet engine planes starting to be used by some of the airlines, but these giants are not jets.

I try not to think about the fact that I don't know what kind of airplane this is. I board the plane, find my seat, and put my overnight bag in the overhead storage. I settle in my seat and try to think of nothing but home and love, at last. Once we are in the air, a short nap should help calm me down. With 2,000 miles and many hours to go, it will probably be a very long one, if I can ever fall asleep.

With all the other passengers finally seated, the pilot announces, "Welcome on board our Lockheed Electra."

He continues with the flight time, the altitude and so on, but I can't hear him. I am still locked onto the words "Lockheed Electra."

For over six months, there have been constant news stories about the Lockheed Electra's wing problems. In fact, above certain speeds, the wings fall off. I feel that old demon, Fear, creeping over me. *With all the crap I have gone through since I first got to Alaska, and then the Arctic, with only hours to go, I don't need to be on a plane with no wings.*

To calm the concerns of the passengers who are aware of the plane's problem, the pilot announces, "Lockheed is aware of the wing problem. Their design engineers have already found the cause and are diligently working on a solution. With certain restrictions, the government is still allowing us to provide you with the fine qualities of this aircraft."

Before I can holler, "What restrictions?" the pilot

explains, "The restriction is that we must fly at a speed somewhat slower than what is normal for high-altitude, cross-country flights like this one."

Already concerned about being late to Chicago, I am again forced to control my mouth, as I want to ask, "What is a 'somewhat slower' speed?"

"We will soon be entering an area of significant thunderstorm activity," the pilot continues. "There is no danger to us, but we will need to alter our course to fly around it. There will also be added head winds. Both of these events will further delay our arrival time in Chicago. Our apologies to all those on connecting flights and to those with family members awaiting your arrival. Our main concern is for your safety. Thank you for your understanding."

All of this "even later" arrival in Chicago talk is not good for my less-than-positive attitude about flying. I remember my concerns about the ancient one-and-a-half engine plane and its aging bush pilot that finally did get me to the Cape, albeit it not too gracefully. At least all the engines on this plane with floppy wings seem to be making their comforting humming sounds.

Trying to look on the bright side, I feel I have accomplished the mission I was sent to do. Annie's and my dream of a better life together is now financially secure and I have tried my best to protect all I love from War. I now know and understand the path I must follow in life.

A strange feeling overcomes me. No longer of Fear but of Love, with a message from a familiar voice, "The past is the past. You have earned your future. It is your destiny to be the light to help others, as I taught you, my eternal friend. I am always with you, as are those who love you."

Yes, I am no longer alone, even though I have felt that way many times in my life. I could not have done all that I have by myself without Annie's love. I know she is waiting for me, no matter how late my return to her will be. I have not totally destroyed my fears and traumatic visions of my dark and violent past but, with her love, I have learned how to control them.

David feels the warmth of Annie's Unconditional Love once again, and he is at last at peace with himself. He feels he no longer must wear the mask of David to cover his fear and guilt. He can now return to his love, Annie, as her Soldier Boy, Wayne.

With this long neglected name at last born again, he still cannot stop worrying about his good friend and his recovery from the Weasel fire on that last day on the mountain.

In his mind, this new Wayne asks his spiritual friends, "What of my good friend who saved me from that charging Caribou on my first day in the Arctic and so many more times after that?"

Many hours and thousands of miles back at the Cape, the medics who examined Eddie knew that there was no rush to bring him down from the mountain. He was already dead from the explosion. They left Eddie in the examination room to go get his records. When they returned, Eddie was gone. There was no trace of his body and there were no records of him in their files. It's as if Eddie had never existed.

Truth About Eddie, Spirits, and George

Still thinking of Eddie, but exhausted from his endless miles of travels and emotional uncertainties, Wayne finally falls into a deep sleep, only to feel a familiar presence.

"Who are you?" he asks.

"For now, think of me as a simple messenger from the divine three, who live as one in your heart and mind."

"Then who is Melvin?"

"Melvin is the first of the three heavenly spirits who came to help you. He is a simple voice of simple words to guide you in your decisions of right and wrong. In your world, you call Him your conscience. In ours, we call Him the Holy Spirit."

"But who is Nanook?"

"Nanook is the second of the three heavenly spirits

who came to help you. I ask of you, Wayne, who is the most loving Father of the universe, the Teacher of wisdom, the source of all forgiveness, strength and beauty? The Creator of life itself?"

"You mean, when I came down from the mountain after almost dying those three days, I saw and was taught by our heavenly Father?"

"Yes, Wayne."

"Eddie is the third of the three heavenly spirits who came to help you. When you went up the mountain on that icy road to save him, you proved you were willing to die for your friend. Yet, it was he who died to save you and the world for a better tomorrow 2,000 years ago. He created a reason for you to make that dangerous journey one last time in a final test of your Free Will when facing impossible choices. There, he gave you one last challenge to battle your dark side, the demon you call WAR, in the form of the stampeding Caribou. As he knew you would, you chose to live. And through the Wisdom you have learned, you will teach others His path of creating a better, loving world, through prayer."

"So, Eddie, my second true friend, who I called my savior when he rescued me from the storm on the mountain, is really my heavenly Savior?"

"Yes, Wayne."

Now, no longer just reacting to Fear, but knowing how to control it to his advantage, the reborn Wayne calls on his dark side, WAR. "Thank you, WAR, for being my friend, for teaching me how to battle against my inner demons and gain the Courage to at last defeat you and understand True Love."

"No! No! Not friendship! Not love!" WAR shouts. "You may have conquered all those fears from me this time with your spiritual friends and ever-growing love, but at the least expected time and place I will be back to test your courage and free will again and again. Who will be with you to protect you then?"

Shaken from his defeat, WAR disappears back into the dark depths of David's subconscious mind only to try to live again, even in David's later life.

Thankful for the countless months of his loving guidance, Wayne asks of his spiritual father, "Michael, are you my spiritual messenger, too?"

"Wayne, I am not the person you called 'Father' who was 'slaughtered by War' as in your vow. He was the father you knew and loved for such a short time before being killed. He was your mother's second love, your stepfather, Steve, who loved you like his own son, when I could not be with you."

Wayne's spiritual father, at last tells him the truth about who he really is, that he has so sadly held back for so long. At last "The Truth Will Set Him Free."

"Wayne, to be with you as you became a true man has been my impossible dream since long ago. You were only one-year-old when I was killed by a train while looking for work and food for my family—your mother, brother, sister, and above all, you.

"While dying, I prayed for a chance to be reborn a better man, and I was. This time, to a poor farming family. In my later years, it was my destiny to leave my parents and the farm. It was my destiny to die again in the army, crawling next to you in the cold Georgia mud as your friend George. Yes, Wayne, my name is truly George, as it was from the beginning, as your father. I knew you had become the son and man I have prayed you would become when you forgave me for deserting you."

Yes, Wayne now knows that whether it was the spirit of his best army friend, George, or that of his spiritual father, Michael, it has been the guiding spirit of his true father all along, searching for his son's forgiveness.

"Father, have I truly made you proud of me? How

could that be when I am so guilty?"

"Wayne, what did you have in your heart when you first began your journey to find the reason for your being, your destiny?"

"Father, I had nothing but Fear, Hate, and the feeling of being in Hell."

"And, now, as your long search is ending, what fills your heart, and even your soul?"

"I found some of George's boundless Courage to control my fears from the dark side of my mind. I have found Annie's Unconditional Love to help me overcome my hate and at last find salvation for of all my guilt over George's death. I no longer believe my being born was the reason you deserted our family, Father."

"Are you not at last the whole, loving, forgiving person you prayed to be?"

"I am trying, and with Annie's help, I believe I am well on my way."

"Wayne, do you feel your sacrifices made a difference in the world?"

"Father, I pray I succeeded in saving all I love, for at least one day, in some small way."

"Then you have answered your own question as to how you have made me so proud of you, my son."

How can Wayne even ask if I am proud of him? I am his father! I was there, feeling him struggle to stay alive, watching him die until True Love resurrected him. I was there when they held the secret ceremony to honor his ability to protect those he loves—his family *and* his nation. What he did those three days changed the world, and not just in "some small way" as Wayne so humbly puts it.

Since the dark Cold War days of 1959 and 1960, when the world was perched on the edge of self-inflicted annihilation, there have been many regional wars. But, never has there been the Global Nuclear War so many had predicted but prayed would never happen. Wayne had revealed to the world the secret he had learned of the Good War. The one that's never allowed to start is the only Good War. Yes, one lone man, Wayne David Evans, did alter the destiny of the entire world.

Of course I am proud of him!

With a bond of understanding and love now formed between them, a talk between a son and his true father begins as never before.

"What name shall we call you now, son?"

"As with the David of old who battled his giant, Goliath, in the many challenges and battles yet to come in my own life, you may also call me David. Yet, in my life of hope and love with Annie, you can call me by my true name, the name you gave me, Father—Wayne David Evans."

Still on the plane of his final journey, Wayne jerks awake from his deep sleep and wonders, *Were all those voices I heard on the plane real, a dream, or just a fantasy from my bewildered imagination?*

Their New Brighter Journey Begins

The pilot announces, "We will soon be starting our descent in preparation for our landing at Chicago's Midway Airport. The weather has cleared enough that you should soon be able to see the city lights in the distance. We apologize for the extended flight time, but your safety is always our primary concern. Thank you for your understanding and thank you for flying on our Lockheed Electra." *Yes, Mr. Pilot, you will certainly have my full understanding when you get these floppy wings safely back on the ground.*

I can now see the welcoming lights of the expressways and, just ahead, the landing lights of the runway coming ever closer towards us. The engine sounds begin to soften, the tires give a gentle bump, and the endless hours of taxiing to the arrival gates begins. After all these many months away, I hope—no, I know—my loved ones have waited just a little longer for me to be back home, especially my Annie.

The last turn, and we come to a gentle stop. I so want to just jump up and rush to the exit, but I can't. I realize others in front of me also want to be with those waiting for them. I tell myself, *I have been away for almost an eternity so a few more minutes won't make any difference*, but I don't believe me.

It's now my turn. My legs, numb from hours of flying, come alive again as I begin to slowly walk down the aisle, but then jerk to a stop. My bag is still in the overhead compartment. I apologize to all those I must squeeze past to get back to my seat and bag. It may contain the only clothes I will have to wear for quite a while if my baggage and gifts are lost forever.

My turn again. I carefully walk down the slippery wet stairs. I firmly plant my feet on solid earth once again. Looking up and through the misty fog, I see someone rushing through the gate towards me. For a fleeting moment my mind rushes back to that day so many months ago when someone else rushed towards me, arms out stretched in a happy greeting. But I then realize it is only a ghostly memory, dissolving into my past of many yesterdays.

This time it is real. It is my beloved Annie rushing to meet me. She stops and looks at me as if I am a stranger. Have I changed that much? With utter disbelief, she realizes it really is me. I have finally come back to her. She hugs me so tightly I can barely breathe, or am I breathless from my final return to our long awaited love? Her kiss is gentle, yet more passionate than I remember. Yes, I am now certain I am back and we are together again.

We catch our breath from the overwhelming excitement and smile at each other. All those passing us, returning to their own loved ones, also smile and plainly hear her as she lovingly looks at me and, almost shouting, tells me one more time how she feels, "At last you are truly back and in my arms once again, my Unconditional Love, my Soldier Boy Wayne."

302

Epilogue

Wayne's true father, George, by his own selflessness in all his roles he played to help Wayne find his true self, has now earned his own destiny. It's the honor of becoming not just an angel, but a Guardian Angel. As Wayne and Annie's personal Guardian Angel, he can be the true father he has always prayed to be.

With Annie's continued help and unconditional love, Wayne David Evans will journey to many more exciting worlds and eventually be known as "the man with more lives than a cat."

Throughout his long life, now known as the author W. D. Evans, he still experiences even greater dark days and sleepless nights than he did in the Arctic.

During his many journeys in his long life, he encounters even greater adventures of survival, including, strokes, concussions and even crashing airplanes four times. He struggles with occasional nights of post-traumatic memories and fear of reliving each battle in his restless mind. Each time, Annie comes to him professing her love.

While searching for a life of meaning and the hidden secret of what creates THE GOOD WAR, he and his lifelong soul mate, Annie, have discovered many times that unconditional love can win over fear.

On some distant day, together, they will feel the breath of their heavenly father as a gentle summer breeze whispering a joyful welcome from above,*"A job well done, My Children, A job well done."*

Some Closing Thoughts:

*"Life is not measured by
the number of breaths we take,
but by the number of moments
that take our breath away."*
Unknown

*"Laugh with Vigor,
Love with Passion,
Dream with Courage."*
W. D. Evans

*"This is Not the End.
This is Not Even
the Beginning of the End.
It May Not Even Be the
End of the Beginning."*
Sr. Winston Churchill

In Honor of a Fellow Soldier and Friend

Sgt. Andrew Fuccillo of Team 7, representing the 75th Ranger Regiment, pushes himself through frigid water and barbed wire in the early morning hours of the 2008 Best Ranger Competition April 18 at Fort Benning, Georgia. Sgt. Fuccillo has gone on to become an Airborne Ranger assistant chaplain with the 75th Ranger Regiment where he is proud to be a Christian Soldier for Jesus.

Original Photo by J. D. Leipold

A Personal Thank You:

Andrew:

I greatly appreciate your allowing me to use your photo to depict the full truth in the bloody dangers of training for the "Slaughter of War."

From the very beginning of my writing efforts, it has been my honor to have you as part of my true life journey from Hate, Fear and Hell, through the threat of Arctic Global Nuclear War, to finally discover Love, Courage and Salvation while "Searching for the Good War."

Although from different times in history, I feel we have formed a bond of brothers. We both struggled to overcome those many agonizing months during our US Army training at Fort Benning, Georgia–training to defend our country in times of a war we prayed would never come. You have gone on to spread inspiration and hope through the words of Jesus Christ as a chaplain. I pray, with the help of the Holy Spirit, I can learn to do the same through my words as an author.

GOD bless you for your continued Belief and Faith in a better world. I pray I may have the privilege of following in your footsteps.

With continued respect, your Fellow Soldier and Friend,

Wayne (W. D. Evans)

Photo Gallery

SEARCHING FOR THE GOOD WAR
Photo Gallery 1

Arctic Friends

Slaughter of War

Last Dance

Parting Kiss

Darkening Tomorrow

49th State

Mighty Bears

Almost There

SEARCHING FOR THE GOOD WAR
Photo Gallery 2

Arctic Isolation

Enemy Warning

Who Took My Tooth?

Dinner Guest

Eddie's Last Trip

Caribou Fear

Wedding Dolls

Unconditional Love

About the Author

Arctic Friends

Wayne D. Evans was born into poverty during the Great Depression. He has learned to escape poverty by reinventing himself as needed so he can support his family and others he mentors in business.

With over 55 years of exciting adventures together, Wayne lives with his lovely wife, Annie, in Milton, Georgia, just outside of Atlanta. Through many difficult times, they are proud of the professional accomplishments of their four children and seven grandchildren. The foundation of his own multiple accomplishments is his loving family.

Wayne is now an author, W.D. Evans, The Man with More Lives Than a Cat™. His first book was *Is It a Bird, a Plane, or a Red Chicken?*. He has developed workshops to accompany *Searching for the Good War*, the second in his Survival X Ten Chronicles. Six additional true-life novels and short stories are scheduled to be added to the series by the end of 2017.

Wayne's philosophy is to live each day to the fullest by helping others.

CPSIA information can be obtained
at www.ICGtesting.com
Printed in the USA
LVOW05*1347091116

512160LV00005B/7/P